"You Never Give Up, Do You?"

Laura felt rage building within her and she met his intense glance, making no attempt to hide her fury. "I don't need or want a man in my life, not ever again. I won't be used for any man's pleasure."

Suddenly, she became aware of the warmth leaping from his body to hers. As their glances merged, his eyes seemed to be melting the coldness within her. His eyes devoured her mouth. As his head lowered slowly toward his goal, he murmured, "What about your own pleasure, Laura? Let me show you how good it can be."

NICOLE MONET

An inveterate writer of romances, Nicole lives in California with her husband and daughter. Writing is her full-time career. "I write," the author says, "because I am a voracious reader, and I feel that in some small way I'm paying back all the pleasure I've received in my lifetime."

Dear Reader:

SILHOUETTE DESIRE is an exciting new line of contemporary romances from Silhouette Books. During the past year, many Silhouette readers have written in telling us what other types of stories they'd like to read from Silhouette, and we've kept these comments and suggestions in mind in developing SILHOUETTE DESIRE.

DESIREs feature all of the elements you like to see in a romance, plus a more sensual, provocative story. So if you want to experience all the excitement, passion and joy of falling in love, then SILHOUETTE DESIRE is for you.

I hope you enjoy this book and all the wonderful stories to come from SILHOUETTE DESIRE. I'd appreciate any thoughts you'd like to share with us on new SILHOUETTE DESIRE, and I invite you to write to us at the address below:

Karen Solem
Editor-in-Chief
Silhouette Books
P.O. Box 769
New York, N.Y. 10019

NICOLE MONET
Love's Silver Web

Silhouette Desire

Published by Silhouette Books New York

America's Publisher of Contemporary Romance

SILHOUETTE BOOKS, a Simon & Schuster Division of
GULF & WESTERN CORPORATION
1230 Avenue of the Americas, New York, N.Y. 10020

ISBN: 0-671-44820-X

First Silhouette Books printing June, 1982

10 9 8 7 6 5 4 3 2 1

Interior design by Joann Foster

America's Publisher of Contemporary Romance

Printed in the U.S.A.

For my little big sister—Sandi,
whose pride in me could never equal
my pride in her

Love's
Silver Web

1

With a jerk Laura's head rose from the pile of folders in front of her to stare in the direction of the buzzing phone. Irritated at the interruption, she was unnecessarily abrupt as she spoke into the receiver.

"Social Welfare, Laura Spencer speaking. May I help you?"

Far from being intimidated by her manner, the man on the other end of the wire laughed, and the husky sound caused the back of her neck to prickle.

"Would it be better if I called back later?" he asked.

Ashamed of her lack of control, she forced herself to respond politely. "Who is speaking, please?"

"My name is Matthews, Miss Spencer, from AET in Berkeley. I'm calling in regard to a man we hired on your recommendation a month ago."

At his mention of AET, the largest distributor of iron castings for heavy machinery in the United States, she straightened her spine. She remembered the man in question, his appearance bordering on gaunt, and his pathetic eagerness to find work. Her father had mentioned the iron foundry indirectly, while extolling the business acumen of the owner. Her parents had met him during a fund-raising dinner for a rising young politician. Since her father was rarely given to praise, the conversation had lingered in her mind. When, during the interview, Mr. Stoneman mentioned foundry experience, it seemed the most natural act of providence, and she had sent him to AET to apply for a job.

"Miss Spencer, I hear you breathing, so I assume you're still there," he muttered, his voice hardening perceptibly.

"I . . . I'm sorry, Mr. Matthews," she replied, anger mingling with mortification at the reprimand. "You're referring to Mr. Stoneman, I presume?"

"You presume correctly," he said, mocking her formality. "What the hell were you thinking of, dropping names to my general manager to influence his decision? I returned from lobbying in Washington to find Stoneman employed, and my general manager smirking at me as if he'd done me a personal favor."

Matthews! Now she remembered her father mentioning the name. She was speaking to the great man himself . . . and she wasn't a bit impressed by his manners!

"Is he a satisfactory employee, Mr. Matthews?" At her interruption, she heard him draw in his breath sharply, and she could almost feel the crackling of his anger over the line.

"Whether he is or isn't is entirely my business, honey. What I'm objecting to is some sneaking little do-gooder trying to put one over on me."

"That's not what I did," she gasped, stiffening with indignation. "My father mentioned you, and I sent Mr. Stoneman over to complete an application. I did nothing underhanded!"

"Giving the impression you and I are . . . friends. You call that nothing?"

His hesitation was insulting, and she bridled at the implication. How dare he? she fumed.

"I don't know where you got your information, but you're way off base. I'm rather choosy in picking my . . . friends," she retorted, "and believe me, you'd be the last person I'd choose. You're hard, and callous, and . . . and totally unfair in your accusations. Your general manager received Mr. Stoneman's basic background from me, nothing else. It was he who asked if I was related to Darryl Spencer, and I admitted to being his daughter. Is it my fault he chose to place his own construction on that?"

"Is your hair red?"

"Wh-what?" Her mouth flew open in surprise at the shift in the conversation, and she wanted to scream with frustration.

"Your mother's a gorgeous blonde, your father a redhead," he murmured. "With your temper, my guess is you take after Darryl."

He had ended their conversation with a deep, shiveringly husky chuckle, and a promised "See you later, honey." Not on your life, mister! Applying herself to her work with renewed diligence, she successfully erased the unpleasant incident from her mind.

The rest of the day passed fairly quickly, and for once she was more than ready to leave when four-thirty rolled around. Normally she worked much later, meeting her roommate, Cheryl, and walking with her to the BART station. Tonight, though, Cheryl was meeting her fiancé, and Laura was nervous about leaving the building alone after dark. Her childishness irritated her, but she could always rationalize it by telling herself she had earned an early night.

The BART terminal was crowded with humanity, and she felt protected in the midst of the surging crowds. As she stood on the open platform, a cold breeze from the bay caused her to pull up the hood of her coat. The whining roar of the speeding train approaching in the distance was greeted by the people around her with enthusiastic relief, and as the doors closed behind her, she, too, sighed with gratitude.

Gray clouds moved and shifted, their formations casting lengthening shadows over the lake set like a jewel in the heart of Oakland's business district. As she stared in fascination at the rippling patterns crossing the surface of the wind-tossed water, Laura struggled to catch her breath.

Checking the watch on her slim wrist, she realized it was past time to retrace her steps to her apartment. A particularly lusty gust of wind buffeted her slight form, and she could smell rain in the air. Where weather was concerned, March wasn't the most predictable of months, but then, California weather was rarely predictable. From the looks of that sky, it wasn't a question of whether it would rain, but when. Well, standing here brooding about the weather really would make her late for work, she thought, quickening once again into a run.

Overheated from running, she didn't welcome the

blast of warm air which greeted her as she entered her apartment. Her tennis shoes made little sound as she crossed the white-and-gold mosaic-tiled entry hall, but she still tiptoed from habit. She didn't want to wake Cheryl before it was absolutely necessary.

Laying her brown wool three-piece suit on her bed, she shrugged. She knew she would be glad of its warmth later, but at the moment it looked far from appealing. With a sigh of relief she stepped out of her blue jogging clothes, carrying them into the bathroom and closing the lid on the hamper with a controlled slam.

Facing her reflection in the mirror, she almost laughed aloud. The cold air had left her face white and pinched-looking, but there was a hectic flush on her high cheek-bones from running, and her nose positively glowed. Combined with green eyes and a wealth of bright red hair, the effect was overpowering.

Laura rushed through bathing and dressing, ever conscious of the steadily moving hands of her watch. Slipping the suit jacket on over the tailored sleeves of a plain eggshell-white blouse, she turned to study her reflection in her dressing-table mirror. Her hair was confined in a knot on the back of her slim neck, stretching tightly against her temples. She felt secure once again in her image, that of a coolly controlled, inconspicuous career woman, and with a final straightening tug at the vest hugging her waist, she went to wake Cheryl.

Nobody would guess that an extremely efficient nurse lurks beneath these covers, she thought, a smile curving her mouth. Of course, even out of the covers Cheryl was a far cry from the image her profession suggested. Petite, with a mass of tightly curled brown hair hugging her scalp, coffee-cream complexion, and gamine grin, Cheryl Blake more closely resembled a little girl than a district welfare nurse.

Shaking the lump in the middle of the bed, Laura was greeted by a muffled groan.

"Come on, lazybones, time to get up."

A tangled bunch of hair became visible as Cheryl crawled slowly toward daylight.

"You have a mean streak in you, Laura," she muttered, clasping her hands over her head and burrowing a turned-up nose in the pillow.

With a final swat at Cheryl's raised derriere, Laura laughingly turned toward the door. "In that case, I won't save you any coffee," she threatened.

"You wouldn't dare!"

"Think not? In twenty minutes your coffee goes down the sink!"

"Cruel, cruel, cruel," Cheryl wailed in a flurry of scattered blankets and honey-brown arms and legs. "I really am going to tell Frank on you this time," she warned, a grin belying her words. "You'll be sorry!"

"Frank's the one who'll be sorry. He's sentencing himself to a lifetime of getting you up in the morning!"

The pillow missed her by inches, and she was still chuckling to herself as she entered the kitchen. As she mechanically prepared coffee and toast, her thoughts centered upon Cheryl's fiancé. Frank Simmons was a tall, darkly handsome young doctor in his last year of residency at Kaiser Hospital in Oakland. They were planning to be married as soon as Frank's residency was finished at the end of the year, and Laura couldn't help envying Cheryl's enthusiasm in planning the wedding.

"Right on time," Cheryl crowed. "Where's that coffee?"

"In front of you!" Laura pointed to a steaming earthenware mug on the counter. "Are you sure you washed all the sleep out of your eyes?"

"How did you know it wouldn't get cold, smart aleck?"

"After three years, I have the routine down pat."

"Oh, what I wouldn't give to be perfect!"

"Shut up and eat your toast."

Much to Laura's disgust, the lowering weather proved prophetic as far as her day was concerned. A phone call from her mother set the seal on her mood.

That's all I needed to make the day perfect, she thought. Sitting back, she flexed her fingers painfully. Massaging her temple in an attempt to ease the throbbing pulsebeat, she closed her eyes against the pain.

Leaning her forehead upon tightly clenched hands, she sighed. Ordinarily the damp March weather wouldn't have bothered her, but today it seemed to deepen her depression. Really, her mother's timing was inspired, she mused, her mouth tightening in exasperation. She always seemed to call when Laura was least able to spend the time arguing, and today had been one of those days.

Normally she loved her job as a social worker, finding her profession extremely rewarding. Of course, among her cases were those who wanted something for nothing, who would make little or no attempt to help themselves, but they were the exception. She had become adept at reading faces as well as statistics, and over the years had found that intuition also played a substantial part in making her final decisions. The most difficult aspect of her job was in hardening herself, keeping the pity she felt for wasted lives buried behind a calmly professional facade.

When she first began her career, she was ready to change the world single-handedly. In those days when some of her more determined efforts met with defeat, she had shuddered under a terrible sense of inadequacy. Slowly, painfully, she had managed to build up her defenses, and now, at nearly twenty-eight, she had learned that to survive meant never becoming personally involved.

Leaning back in her chair, she gazed through the glassed-in cubicle partition which separated her from the outer office. She had started her career out there five years ago, after receiving her degree from the University of California at Berkeley and passing the Civil Service requirements for employment.

Through her years at the university she'd worked hard to get the best grades possible. It hadn't taken long for invitations to parties and other amusements to stop being offered. Her fellow students, both male and female, quickly dubbed her a stuck-up bore, and even now the memory was painful. They hadn't understood her desire, which was almost obsessive, to succeed in carving out a future for herself . . . by her own efforts.

For too many years she'd enjoyed the best of everything—the most expensive clothes, exclusive schools. Returning home from boarding school after graduation, she hadn't raised much fuss when her mother requested she delay entering a university, and accompany her on a cruise. The idea appealed to her, and she was used to indulging her fancies. At eighteen she was too young and thoughtless to have had much inner direction. She hadn't known then how drastically her life would change as a result of that trip. It was there, during glorious sun-filled days and romantic nights of moonlight and music, that she met Phillip.

Thoughts of the nightmare that had been her marriage seared through her. Shivering, she wrapped her arms about herself in a curiously defensive gesture as she rose to stand beside the window. Staring out at the rain-washed streets, she suddenly longed to be walking beside the lake once again, with Kaiser Center curving majestically upward from Lakeshore Drive. She needed to feel the damp breezes on her cheeks while she watched the ripples forming on the water from the lashing rain.

Clenching her fingers on the windowsill, she rested her forehead against the glass, the coolness and the smell of the rain reviving her somewhat.

There wouldn't be time for the walk she longed for, and she couldn't help feeling irritated. Once again she had let her mother maneuver her, and now she was committed to spending the evening with her parents. There hadn't been any way she could sidestep the invitation. When she tried, her mother's tearful pleadings had left her tongue-tied. Dear Lord! She had worked so hard to achieve her own individuality, to recover from the self-destructive course she had inadvertently plotted for herself.

Considering her sophisticated upbringing, she had been curiously innocent at eighteen. It was only after it was too late that she finally faced the truth. She had been no more than the means to an end for the man she had married, a way for him to enjoy the good life he craved, without having to work for it.

Her sweetly ineffectual mother, visions of grandchildren dancing in her head, had fallen prey to Phillip's practiced manner as quickly as Laura had, and was little or no protection. As for her father, Phillip could have had two heads for all the attention he paid to his daughter's fiancé.

They were married within a month of her return from the cruise. Laura accompanied her new husband to her parents' upon returning from their honeymoon. As she entered her former home that evening, she had been older and wiser, with a hard core of bitterness already forming within her. His behavior during the hours which followed sickened her, as he quite obviously fawned upon her family. Once, meeting her father's eyes and seeing he was making no attempt to hide his contempt, she felt herself burning with shame and resentment. He had been too busy to guide her as a father should, so he had no right to sit in judgment now, she remembered thinking.

It hadn't taken her father's derisive attitude to make the scales fall from her eyes where her husband was concerned. Phillip quite successfully accomplished the unveiling himself, she thought, biting her lip with remembered pain and degradation. During their honeymoon she discovered the true nature of the man she'd married, quickly realizing that his surface charm hid a self-centeredness which appalled her. He was petulant and surly when things didn't go his way, which was often. Phillip thrived on constant attention and adulation. His ego was monumental, his concentration on himself complete. Within a week he callously admitted his mercenary reasons for marrying her; he'd been displeased because she had objected to his embarrassing behavior toward one of the maids. Eventually she learned to retreat

18

behind a wall of pride, unable to bear the pity she often saw directed toward her.

Sighing, Laura turned back toward her desk, her lips pressed together in a taut line. With grim purpose she once more lowered her head to the open file before her, only to groan in defeat when the words blurred on the page. Closing her eyes tiredly, she was unaware of the door opening until she heard footsteps coming toward her, echoing hollowly on the yellowed linoleum surface.

"Really, Laura! You're a glutton for punishment, do you know that?"

With scant regard for the condition of Laura's desktop, Cheryl pushed a pile of papers aside and sat down, her feet swinging back and forth childishly. Grasping the folder from Laura's hands, Cheryl snapped it shut. "Come on, time to go home."

"I only have a few more notations to make. It's early yet!"

"Are you kidding? It's after six o'clock. Everybody else left long ago."

Gasping with surprise, Laura glanced at the white-faced regulation clock on the far wall. "I've done it again, haven't I?"

"After all this time, I guess I'm used to it"—Cheryl laughed—"but enough is enough. Anyway, since Frank's on duty tonight, I thought we were eating out."

Laura had forgotten her suggestion, and gazed guiltily upward. Apologizing, she explained about her mother's invitation, and Cheryl nodded in understanding.

As Laura tidied her desk, carefully replacing her folders in a green metal filing cabinet in the corner, Cheryl's light chatter flowed around her soothingly.

"There you go again, Laura, off in your own world,"

Cheryl complained. "I bet you haven't heard a word I've been saying."

"Yes I have. You were telling me Frank's been offered a place on the staff after he finishes his residency. I'm just not surprised, that's all." Laughing at Cheryl's proud expression, Laura turned to hug her. "I'm so happy for you both. I know how much you wanted to stay in the Bay Area. I'll bet your families are jumping with joy."

"We haven't told them yet, but I know Mama will be relieved. She sure didn't like the idea of her only daughter moving away." She chuckled, standing up and stretching in contentment. "I didn't want to move, either. I've put too much time into my job, for one thing. Anyway, much as I hate to admit it, I'm rather fond of this town, even on a lousy day like today."

"What a shame you and Frank can't go out tonight to celebrate. And now I've let you down at the last minute, too."

"Don't worry about it. Frank and I will have the rest of the weekend to celebrate." Cheryl's voice was mischievous as she followed Laura from the office. "It'll be a relief to go straight home without enduring a wrestling match first. That man's an animal!"

Laura was glad her back was turned at that moment. Taking longer to lock her door than was necessary, she fought to control the hectic flush staining her cheeks. She wasn't shocked by her friend's words—far from it. The fact that Cheryl's comment embarrassed her caused her momentary worry. Was she turning into an old-fashioned spinster, for heaven's sake?

As they walked down the hall, Laura adjusted the waistband of her skirt. Until Cheryl spoke, she wasn't paying much attention to her surroundings.

"This place gives me the creeps after everyone's gone." Cheryl eyed the dingy hallway in disgust. "You'd think they could have painted the walls anything but this ugly color."

Laura, too, looked at the unattractive green two-tone walls. "I have my own theories about that," she laughed.

"Well, if you have a reason why this floor is the only one in the building decorated with such flair, please let me in on it. All the other private business offices have that gorgeous gold carpeting and lemon-yellow walls. The corridor on the main floor even has wallpaper," Cheryl complained.

As they entered the elevator, the large, cumbersome doors closed on the sight Cheryl found so offensive, and Laura's slanting green eyes gleamed impishly. "You know how fond the Army is of green?" she questioned. "My idea is that some general, probably around World War II, went crazy mixing paints together. The end result was that sickly color, and even though they cashiered him, the harm was done. They had so much of the stuff left over, they're still trying to get rid of it!"

"Now I know why all county offices look alike! Even the hospitals manage to retain that same rustic flavor." Cheryl grinned, finally bursting out in a pealing laugh. "You're a genius!"

"I know," Laura sighed. They stepped out of the elevator into a carpeted foyer, the pale yellow walls lined with impressionistic paintings.

"Now, this is more like it," Cheryl said.

Dropping her purse on a white leather bench, Laura put on her brown trench coat, belting the waist tightly and pulling the hood up to cover her hair.

"It's a shame," Cheryl muttered, staring at Laura

intently. "Why do you pull your hair back in that tight knot? You look like a prim schoolteacher, especially when you wear those tailored suits, with your blouses buttoned right to the top."

They had been over this territory before, so Laura just brushed Cheryl's words aside. "I dress for comfort, not sex appeal," she laughed, slinging her shoulder bag into position.

"You mark my words," Cheryl warned, her large, soulful eyes earnest. "One day some guy is going to see through all these barriers you protect yourself with. He's going to blow all your defenses sky-high, and there won't be a thing you can do about it."

"I'd like to see anyone try! You know what I went through in my marriage. I'll never give another man the chance to use me again. All Phillip wanted was an adoring slave, and he only married me because he thought a wealthy father-in-law would be useful."

"Not all men are like that, Laura."

With a sigh, Laura admitted the truth in her friend's assertion. Once in a while, because she needed an escort to a particular function, or at Cheryl's instigation, she dated. Some of the men had been pleasant. Eventually, though, they tried furthering the relationship. As soon as this happened, she refused to have anything more to do with them—and she never regretted it. She was her own woman now, and saw no reason why she should suffer attentions distasteful to her. "I guess I don't much like men," she remarked bitterly, turning from Cheryl's compassionate gaze. "At least, that's what Phillip always told me . . . and anyone else who would listen."

"He was an unfeeling . . . Well, you've heard my opinion of your husband before, I don't need to repeat myself. The best thing he ever did for you was running off with that filthy-rich widow and giving you your freedom. You're a warm and loving person underneath that wall you've built around yourself, and it makes me sick to see that warmth going to waste!"

"Hey, it's all in the past," Laura exclaimed. "I'm perfectly happy now, so why are you getting so upset?"

"Because he scarred you, and you know it. Not all men are out for what they can get," she replied, tightening the belt of her duffel coat with jerky movements.

"No, but I could never be sure," Laura murmured, following Cheryl out of the building. Consciously banishing memories of Phillip into the past, she lifted her face until the wind-buffeted raindrops cooled her heated flesh. Laughing aloud at a comment from Cheryl, she felt the blood coursing through her veins in tune to the lash of the moisture stinging her cheeks.

With ease born of long practice, Laura negotiated the twisting turns in the hills high above the university town of Berkeley. With a murmur of relief she turned onto the private road which led to her old home. The house, as she feared it would be, was ablaze with lights. Thinking this would turn out to be another of her mother's interminable parties, she fought the urge to turn around and leave. Common sense reasserted itself when she noticed the absence of other vehicles parked along the circular drive. Swallowing with difficulty, she parked underneath the redwood carport.

There was an entry from the carport into a slate-floored vestibule, but Laura chose to use the front entrance. She walked gingerly in the black suede pumps she had chosen to go with the ankle-length skirt she wore. Also of suede, it molded her figure closely, a side split giving tantalizing flashes of a long, slender leg as she moved.

As she reached the top of the stairs, the scent of the pine and eucalyptus trees surrounding the house brought forth a deluge of memories, not all of them pleasant. There had been too much loneliness in her childhood, too many days spent playing by herself. As if to remind her of things forgotten, the wind sighed through the trees overhead. To her fervent imagination, it seemed as if the sound were mourning the child she had been, or possibly the woman she had become.

"Miss Laura, how wonderful to see you again!" Emma held the door open wide in welcome, her round, aging face glowing with pleasure as she took Laura's coat.

"Emma, you look great," Laura cried, throwing her arms around the woman who had been housekeeper and friend since she could remember. "How have you been?"

"Fine, Miss Laura, just fine. My, it's certainly good to have you home. It's been much too long since your last visit."

Laura nodded, her eyes rueful. "I know, I've been behaving rather childishly, but I was so furious with Mother for surprising me with that party. Between Mother's well-intentioned matchmaking and Father's air of aloof amusement, I swore I'd never come back. Thank goodness there's nothing in the works for tonight."

Emma's eyes were troubled as she squeezed Laura's arm in silent communication.

"Laura, is that you?" Irene Spencer's voice drifted down from the balcony overhead, her tone petulant.

"For heaven's sake, we're waiting to start dinner. You can gossip with Emma some other time."

Passing Emma with a look of apology, Laura saw the familiar impersonal mask descending upon the other woman's face, and she sighed with regret. Mother has always been jealous of my relationship with Emma, she thought. Emma had practically raised her during her childhood. To her father, business had been all-important. Building the large industrial conglomerate he now headed had entailed extensive traveling, and he had insisted his wife accompany him whenever possible. As Laura slowly maneuvered the stairs, she wondered once again why the two people waiting for her had ever bothered to have a child.

She had inherited her mother's classical bone structure, but looking up at her father, she decided there could be no doubt as to where she had gotten her vivid coloring. At fifty-nine, he was still an amazingly youthful-looking man. His thick red hair was slightly darker than his daughter's, its brightness only partially subdued by a slight smattering of gray.

"Hello, Mother," Laura smiled. "I'm sorry I'm late. How are you, Father?"

"Do you really care?"

Laura winced at his mocking words, refusing to lower her jade eyes from his lighter, and somehow colder, green ones. "Does it matter?" she replied, her voice as toneless as she could make it.

"Laura, you know your father's only teasing," Irene murmured nervously. "Come and sit in front of the fire, dear. You must be frozen."

Laura stepped down into a circular conversation pit.

Her feet sank into thick white carpeting, which contrasted startlingly with the powder-blue furniture. Only Mother would have insisted upon a Ben Franklin stove in white, she thought in amusement as she seated herself before its warmth.

"You've redecorated since I've been here," she murmured, her eyes scanning the large room desultorily.

"Yes, I've found the most marvelous decorator, darling. Do you like it?" At Laura's nod, Irene beamed.

"How's that job of yours going?" her father asked.

She replied politely, retreating farther into the shell she had learned to surround herself with when dealing with her parents.

Laura became aware of footsteps just moments before Emma's voice broke the uneasy silence which had fallen. "Mr. Matthews has arrived, sir."

"Thank you, Emma. That will be all for the present." As he spoke, Darryl Spencer moved, his hand outstretched. "Jace, glad you could make it."

Laura felt rage building within her as the pieces of the puzzle fell into place. Now she no longer had to wonder why her mother had been so insistent that she dine with them tonight. Laura's voice shook as she muttered, "You never give up, do you?"

2

~~~~~~~~~~~~~~~~~~~~

I haven't the slightest idea what you mean. Really, Laura! Must you always let your imagination run away with you?"

Standing, Laura clenched her hands at her sides, doing her best to ignore the familiar masculine voice behind her. "I suppose it's just a coincidence, like the last time?"

"Well . . . not exactly," Irene admitted, looking slightly shamefaced. "Jace dropped by last night, and mentioned speaking to you over the phone. He seemed interested in meeting you, so I thought, since he was coming to dinner anyway . . ." Her voice trailed off in dismay as she noticed Laura's increasing anger. "Darling, there's absolutely no reason to get so upset. Jace is here mainly to discuss business. He and your father's firm are collaborating to complete a particularly large government order, and they wanted to discuss the details in comfort."

"In that case, they'll probably have much to discuss, Mother. I'd only be in the way, and suddenly I'm not very hungry."

"Laura!" The quaver in her mother's voice was unmistakable, and Laura hesitated from force of long habit. Turning, she stared into remorseful blue eyes, and felt the old, familiar sense of defeat assail her.

When her father beckoned her, she almost felt relieved. Anything to break the rather uneasy silence which had fallen. Her face a calm mask, she walked toward him, to be introduced to his guest. She was only vaguely aware of broad shoulders tapering to slim hips and powerful thighs. At her approach, however, he turned to look at her, and she nearly gasped in shock. While her father performed the introductions, she could feel her breathing constrict in her chest. Black hair lay in thick waves against a well-shaped head, while startling wings of white fanned his temples. The man was all contrast, she thought. White on black, framing a face stamped with harshness, yet with a full lower lip which hinted at a core of deep sensuality.

It was his eyes, though, which filled her with uneasiness. Eyes as gray and cool as a San Francisco fog seemed to pierce hers, then moved downward slowly in obvious masculine appraisal. That he liked what he saw was evident by the softening of his mouth, as his gaze once again returned to her face.

Laura thanked whatever fates prevailed when she was seated across from him during dinner. She couldn't have stood a closer proximity. As if he could read her mind, his lips curved in a mocking smile, while his eyes conveyed a subtle message, going meaningfully to her hair. Looking at him challengingly, she was glad he couldn't see the angry curling of her fingers beneath the table.

He was the perfect guest, she thought later. With a

finesse of which she was unaware at the time, he drew her out, questioning her about her work at the welfare agency, and appearing fascinated with her replies. Far from being flattered by his attention, she found herself wishing she had kept quiet. She felt threatened whenever he looked at her, and she had to consciously stop herself from squirming under his regard.

Her expression becoming as sour as her thoughts, she glared at him. With determination she deliberately turned her head to talk with her mother. She clenched her hands tighter than before, furious when she heard his muffled laugh before he resumed his earlier conversation with her father.

Dinner was served, but she wasn't aware of what she was eating. Her mouth seemed perpetually dry, and she sipped carelessly at her wine.

"What are your plans for your birthday next week?" her mother was asking, interested as always in the social side of life. "We could have a little celebration. . . ."

"No, I don't think so, but thanks anyway, Mother. You know I'm not big on celebrations."

"Darling, you've hardly touched your meal. Aren't you feeling well?"

"N-no, I . . ." she stammered. The flush engendered by several glasses of wine on an empty stomach increased. Alcohol certainly wasn't to be trusted as a confidence booster, she realized. As Jace's eyes met hers, any confidence she still retained slowly drained away.

"Perhaps you'd feel better with some fresh air, Laura." His words were more of an order than a question, and before she could protest, her mother happily seconded the invitation.

"Yes, it's rather warm in here, Jace," she remarked, smiling widely. "Laura, why don't you show Mr. Matthews the view from the deck?"

Irene's pleased glance passed from her daughter to Jace, and knowing her mother, Laura decided she was probably envisioning the looks her grandchildren might inherit. A sudden image of a small red-haired, silver-eyed child floated through her mind, and she stiffened in shock.

As Jace followed her through the sliding glass doors onto the redwood balcony, she wished she hadn't been stupid enough to drink so much. Swaying slightly in the cool evening air, she was startled when hard arms pulled her momentarily against an even harder body.

Something within her seemed to snap. All at once she felt fear curling her stomach at the pressure of muscled thighs against her softer curves.

"Don't touch me!" Twisting away from him, she turned like a cornered animal. She wanted to laugh at the stunned expression on his face, only it wasn't at all funny. Her words had been instinctive, as instinctive as her violent reaction to his touch. As his eyes narrowed consideringly, she flinched at the impression she was creating. Why in the world had she overreacted like that? Taking a deep breath, she moved to the railing. "I'm sorry, Mr. Matthews. That was unforgivably rude of me."

"Why?"

At the question, she faced him, her eyes startled. "Why what?" She almost cringed at the harshness of her voice. What right did he have to question her? Ever since their phone conversation, she had taken an active dislike to him, but surely that was her prerogative? It had nothing to do with his appearance, for he was a blatantly attractive man, if not conventionally handsome. His face was too forceful, too obviously masculine for mere good looks, she thought. Maybe that was the problem. She probably resented the aura of powerful control he exuded, not the man himself. She congratulated herself on the logic of her deductions, but her relief was short lived.

"Why do you dislike being touched by me, Laura?"

"Did you expect me to throw myself in your arms on the strength of a single phone conversation?" she sneered. "I suppose you find this situation you've created vastly amusing, but pardon me if I don't laugh. Maybe most women respond to your debatable charms, Mr. Matthews, but I don't happen to be one of them. I just don't like being pawed by a perfect stranger. My taste in men must be more discriminating than you planned on," she mocked, enjoying the sight of the anger tightening his face. "The fact that you're a wealthy man, used to being flattered and fawned over, doesn't impress me in the least. The sad truth is, Mr. Matthews . . . you simply don't appeal to me."

"Stop trying to cover up," he ordered. "You have to admit my casual touch didn't warrant the violence of your response."

"I haven't the slightest idea what you mean," she replied, her voice cold.

"Don't you?" Jace murmured the words while making a determined move forward, and Laura's hard-won poise faded. If he came any closer, she felt she would shatter into a thousand pieces, and her face paled at the thought.

His mouth was a taut white line as her eyes locked with his. When she saw compassion in their depths, a scorching sense of shame enveloped her. She was trapped within molten silver, which burned through her flesh and invaded the inner recesses of her mind. It was as if he saw her more clearly than she could see herself; the knowledge was there in his eyes. This stranger had pierced her hard-won defenses effortlessly, seeing what she preferred to keep hidden, and she hated him for it!

With a cry Laura brushed past him, unable to bear his closeness a moment longer. An impression of her mother's startled face floated within her consciousness, but she was incapable of offering any explanations. Stopping only long enough to grab her purse, she ran down the stairs as if the devil himself were following, as indeed he was, in her estimation.

She never could remember much about the drive home. She moved mechanically, her thoughts turned inward. Only later, as she lay shivering beneath the covers of her bed, did she berate herself for the childishness of her actions. As she slid into sleep, she once again saw Jace running toward her car, his voice crying her name. Then the image became mixed with her dreams.

Late-morning sunlight poured through the window, its light beating against her closed eyelids. With a groan she burrowed her head in the pillow, finally giving in with a grumble of defeat.

In an attempt to obliterate the memory of piercing silver eyes, she sat up in bed and surveyed the room. How pretty the drapes looked, with the sunlight pouring between their folds, to cast shifting patterns on the deep burgundy velvet. Running her fingers over the matching bedspread, she realized she was not reacting to the rich texture with her usual degree of pleasure, and experienced a return of anger from the evening before. With disgust at her flagging spirits, she jumped from the bed, determined that thoughts of that black-haired devil shouldn't ruin what promised to be a lovely day.

While the bath filled, she straightened the bedroom. Smoothing the last wrinkle, she crossed to the walk-in closet which took up most of one wall, withdrawing blue denims, her normal housecleaning garb. Throwing them carelessly upon the bed, she rummaged through her drawers in search of a top. This accomplished, she grabbed minuscule cotton-and-lace bikini underwear and returned to the bathroom.

Laying the panties on the white tile counter, she raised her eyes to study her reflection in the tile-to-ceiling mirror. With a grimace of distaste at the almost abandoned sensuality of her image, she resisted the urge to lower her eyes, and instead studied herself with a sensation of detachment. The fiery red tresses rippling nearly to her waist and the ivory-skinned body almost totally revealed by the wispy nylon nightgown she wore hardly seemed to belong to her.

At times she wondered if she had a split personality. At this thought, her expression became grim as she began piling her hair on top of her head, her movements uncoordinated. This stranger reflected in the mirror was a woman she kept hidden from everyone but Cheryl—a woman who loved frothy, dainty garments next to her skin, who delighted in the feel of long wavy hair down her back. The other Laura was a pitiful contrast, a prim, severely dressed woman whose appearance manifested her reserved personality.

Dropping the clinging folds of her gown at her feet, she deliberately avoided her naked image. Turning off the flow of water into the tub, she gingerly tested the temperature with her toes. Gasping at the heat, she nevertheless stepped fully into the bath, and as her skin became accustomed to the warmth, she lay back with a sigh of relief.

As she allowed her mind and body to relax, a forbidden face seemed to float into her mind. She remembered mahogany-tan skin stretched smoothly over high cheekbones, dark brows shading deeply set pools of silver promise. When that last thought manifested itself, a shiver of awareness coursed through her, as unexpected as it was unwelcome.

Jerking upright in the rapidly cooling water, she frowned. So much for good resolutions, she thought with disgust. For some reason she was loath to explain, Jace Matthews's image refused to be banished. Using a bar of gardenia-scented soap, she scrubbed furiously, rubbing her skin harder than necessary to rid herself of the strange tingling she was experiencing. After releasing the water from the tub, she stood and adjusted the hand-shower nozzle to a fine cold spray, which not only rinsed the clinging soap from her body but also dispelled the last of her inertia.

Leaving the bath towel tucked securely around her slightly damp body, she efficiently tidied the bathroom. After brushing her teeth and putting on the minimum of makeup, she slipped into her panties. She never wore a bra, disliking the feeling of restriction. Luckily her breasts were very firm, so the omission wasn't noticeable.

The bathroom once again in its usual pristine condition, Laura closed the door behind her. Going over to the bed, she dressed hurriedly. As she released her hair from the carelessly executed coil on her head, she dropped the pins on the white surface of her French-provincial dressing table. Fastening it back with a length of ribbon, she felt comfortably capable of tackling the numerous house-hold chores which awaited her.

By eleven-thirty the most onerous tasks were behind her, and Laura decided a meal should be next on the agenda. The small but compact kitchenette had a warm and restful appearance as the sun poured through the casement window, and she looked around her with pleasure. Cream-and-gold walls were beautifully comple-mented by a lovely mosaic-tile floor. The bar alcove opened into a little-used dining room; she and Cheryl preferred to eat informally, unless they had guests.

As if on cue, Laura heard the sound of Cheryl's key in the lock. Thinking she'd need help with the groceries, she hurried into the hall, stopping in surprise when Frank's lanky frame entered behind Cheryl.

"Phew! We must have stood in line for an hour," Cheryl complained, a weighty shopping bag in each arm.

"Here, let me take one of those." Suiting action to words, Laura grabbed the brown parcel which seemed most in danger of spilling its contents upon the floor. Making her way into the kitchen, she threw a smiling hello to Frank, who followed the two women with a long-suffering look on his face.

Strewing the contents of the bags upon any available surface, Laura and Cheryl made short work of putting the groceries away. Frank perched happily on a stool, not a bit upset at being told by his fiancée that he was more of a hindrance than a help.

"Poor Frank," Laura sympathized. "Why you want to marry a woman who doesn't appreciate your better nature, I'll never understand."

A white-toothed grin speared across his features, star-tling in the darkness of his face, and she found herself grinning back unreservedly. His eyes returned to Cheryl as if by instinct, and she felt a lump forming in her throat at the tenderness of his expression. An unfamiliar feeling of envy stole over her, catching her unaware. Shocked at finding herself wondering what it would be like to have a man love her the way Frank obviously loved Cheryl, she turned toward the refrigerator in an attempt to hide her agitation.

"Does either of you want any lunch?" she questioned, quirking an eyebrow in inquiry.

"No thanks, Laura," Cheryl answered, her words muffled as she attempted to shove a box of cereal on a shelf too high for her to reach.

"Here, honey. Let me do that for you." While Frank obligingly placed the box in place, Cheryl leaned back against his steady frame, turning her head to wink at Laura.

Stifling her laughter, Laura moved away, busily preparing her sandwich. She didn't need to see to know what was happening over there in the corner. Obviously Cheryl knew ways of appreciating Frank's sterling qualities which her fiancé thoroughly enjoyed.

Cheryl approached just as Laura was finishing the last bite. "Gee, that looks good," she murmured. "I'm starving."

"It won't take a minute to fix another one. When you turned down my offer of lunch I took it for granted you two had already eaten."

"We didn't have time," Cheryl groaned, clutching her stomach dramatically. "That beast over there showed up at practically the break of dawn, and didn't even give me time for a cup of coffee. He's promised his mother we'd come for lunch, since I told mine we'd go over there for dinner. But for now he's letting me starve to death as punishment for making him help with the groceries."

"Cheryl, I could have done the shopping this week." Laura frowned. "Why didn't you wake me?"

"Look, we share the chores, right? This was your Saturday for cleaning the apartment and mine for getting the groceries. I'm not pushing the full burden on your shoulders, willing though they are. Anyway, I heard you tossing and turning last night. You needed your sleep."

Touched at the concern in her friend's voice, Laura started to reply when she was stopped by the sound of the doorbell.

"I'll get it, Laura," Frank offered, already halfway across the hall. "While I'm gone, would you pour that squalling brat a glass of milk to tide her over? It would be just like her to embarrass me by fainting on my mother's doorstep."

Since the last sentence was yelled from the hall, Frank was spared the sight of his beloved sticking her tongue out at him. Meeting Laura's eyes, Cheryl began to giggle, and soon Laura found herself joining in.

"Hey, Laura," bellowed Frank. "There's somebody here to see you."

Cheryl, her curiosity piqued, followed close behind as Laura entered the living room. She was totally unprepared for Laura's sudden halt at first sight of her guest, and went cannoning into Laura's back, nearly knocking both of them down, much to Frank's unrestrained amusement.

"Laura, what's the matter with you?"

Not bothering to answer her disgruntled friend, she could only stare in horrified fascination at the man standing beside Frank. He seemed to dwarf the large

37

room, and she found she was having an unusual amount of difficulty controlling her breathing.

"Hello, Laura," Jace murmured. "You left in such a . . . hurry last night, you forgot your coat. I offered to bring it by."

After thanking him politely, she was forced into performing the necessary introductions. She avoided Cheryl's questioning eyes, smoothing her hair back with a nervous hand. While Frank and Cheryl began a desultory conversation, Laura attempted to look interested, although she hadn't heard a word. Just the sound of his voice seemed to trigger a defensive mechanism through her brain, and she found herself trembling uncontrollably.

To her horror, she saw Frank and Cheryl going to the door. Surely they weren't going to just leave her alone with this . . . this . . . Apparently that was exactly their intention. With a wave and a last murmured good-bye, they closed the door behind them, and she was left standing in frozen disbelief.

Steeling her shattered nerves, Laura turned to face her unwelcome guest. Some of her resentment must have shown on her face, and she flushed slightly in embarrassment. She could swear she glimpsed amusement in his eyes, and she felt indignant at his ability to reduce her to a gauche schoolgirl.

Moistening her lips, she moved forward to take her coat from his unresisting grasp. With a mumbled apology she turned toward the entry hall. As she placed the coat on a hanger, she could almost feel his eyes boring into her back. The silence was becoming oppressive, and she had to take a deep breath before once again returning to the living room.

"W-would you like a cup of coffee, Mr. Matthews?" She hated herself for allowing her voice to reflect her disquiet. Above all else, she must keep from him the knowledge of how strongly he disturbed her. She could just imagine the construction he would place upon *that* little bit of weakness!

"Thank you, I'd love a cup." A smile lit his features, confusing her into uttering further inanities. What in the world was wrong with her? She was usually well able to control her reactions to the people she met, especially the men!

"Do you mind if I make myself comfortable, Laura? I've spent a rather restless night."

"Not at all," she replied, disturbed herself by the cryptic note in his voice. It was as if he were trying to convey something to her, but she wasn't in any mood to play charades. "Just make yourself at home, Mr. Matthews."

Her hands were none too steady as she prepared the coffee. From the living room came the sounds of a favorite album, and she became clumsy with anger. He certainly believed in taking her at her word, she thought. What had possessed her to utter such a ridiculous statement? The last thing she wanted was for him to make himself at home in her apartment!

Twisting the kitchen faucet with more force than necessary, she uttered a strangled gasp as water splattered the front of the sleeveless knit top she wore. Taking a deep breath and counting to ten, she jumped at the sound of his voice from the doorway.

"Do you need any help?"

The ineffectual dabbings at her soaked top ceased abruptly, and she fought down an irrational urge to burst into tears. She noticed his mouth quirk when he spied the pool of water at her feet. If he makes a sound, I'll throw something at him, she vowed, gripping her teeth together.

"I'm perfectly capable of making coffee, Mr. Matthews!"

"If you say so," he murmured, staring from her to the floor meaningfully. Clenching her hands to prevent herself from hurling the coffeepot at him, she almost lost the battle completely when he turned and threw over his shoulder, "The name's Jace, honey."

Spilling more of the aromatic grounds on the counter than she managed to get in the pot, she seethed. The nerve of the man! Wiping up the mess while she waited for the pot to finish perking, she was glad of the opportunity to work off some of her anger. She was playing right into his hands by showing so little control, and she was determined that, from now on, she would remain unmoved. He was only amusing himself with her, but she was darned if she'd pander to his egotistical urgings. As soon as he drank his coffee, he could go, and good riddance!

Laura prepared two mugs with the steaming liquid. Carrying them into the living room, she almost dropped the tray in stunned amazement. Jace was sprawled cross-legged on the floor, dark brown slacks a perfect foil for the gold carpeting. His snugly fitting green turtleneck emphasized bulging muscles in his arms as he shifted through her record collection. He certainly looks as if he's planning a lengthy visit, but he'll just have to think again, she thought.

"Do you take cream and sugar, Mr. Matthews?"

"Black will be fine," he remarked, his tone absent-minded. "Tell me, Laura, do you have something against my name?"

Lowering her eyes to the earthenware mug in her hands, she hesitated before replying. If she wanted to convince him of her nonchalance, she was going about it in the wrong way, she realized.

"I'm sorry, but it isn't easy for me to become familiar on such short acquaintance . . . Jace." Her composed explanation pleased her enormously, and she hid a smile by taking a sip of coffee.

Getting to his feet in one lithe movement, he stretched in contentment. Against her will her eyes were drawn toward the motion of his stretching form, and she choked when his sweater rose to reveal a taut, flat stomach. She was fascinated by a shadowy furrow of black hair, her eyes following its path hypnotically, until it disappeared within the waistband of his slacks.

Regaining her breath with difficulty, she unconsciously moistened her lips with the tip of her tongue. She felt frozen, unable to coordinate her thoughts or movements as she raised dazed eyes to his face. To her consternation, she noticed that his attention appeared to be concentrated upon her moistened lips, and she shivered at the awareness briefly darkening his eyes.

She felt rather than saw him move. She had placed his mug on the other side of the sculptured-driftwood glass-topped coffee table, as far away from her own as possible. The chocolate-brown divan fanned out in two jutting wings in front of a panoramic view of Lake Merritt below. The only other furniture in the room was the stereo in the corner. She could feel herself beginning to tremble as he quietly lifted his coffee and moved to sit beside her.

"Th-the view is much clearer from over there," she stammered, trying to remain unaffected by his closeness.

His next remark did nothing to dispel her frustration, especially when he casually draped his arm along the back of the divan, his fingers momentarily brushing against her neck. "The view is superb from where I'm sitting," he murmured. "Has anyone ever told you you're incredibly beautiful?"

His voice was husky. Sliding to the edge of her seat, she placed her empty mug on the coffee table. Her back was stiffly unresponsive, his words striking an unwelcome chord of memory in her. Intending to shock him, she met his intense glance, making no attempt to hide her contempt.

"They've tried, Mr. Matthews, but I wasn't disposed to listen. The last man I listened to was my ex-husband, and I paid dearly for it. In the beginning, he used pretty words, until he got what he wanted. You and Phillip would have gotten along famously, I think. He didn't care about me as a person any more than you do, though since you already have money, I assume you have different motives for pursuing me. I'll put this bluntly: I want to be left alone, do you understand?"

Once started, she couldn't seem to stop, and Laura shocked herself rather than him. For too many years she had kept the hatred locked within, and now she was powerless to stop the flow.

She had no strength left to fight as his arms reached around her, pulling her back against the warmth of his chest.

"Feel better?" The gentle question was accompanied by a strong hand brushing the hair from her dampened temples.

"Please . . . I . . . " she stammered, pulling away from him in embarrassment. "After he left, I wanted to wipe out every trace of him from my life. I became independent, and after the divorce I legally reverted to using my maiden name. I don't need or want a man in my life, not ever again. I won't be used for any man's pleasure, Mr. Matthews!"

"What about your own pleasure, Laura?"

Laughing hysterically, she almost cried out in shock when his hands tightened punishingly on her arms.

"Dammit! Quit fighting me," he ordered, forcing her head up to meet his eyes. At his expression of suppressed fury, she began to shake with reaction. She was alone with a virtual stranger—a stranger who at this moment looked as if he would strangle her.

"God, don't look at me like that!" His face had whitened in reaction to her fear. There was a tiny pulse beating in his temple, and suddenly her terror disappeared. It seemed to make him more vulnerable, somehow, and she quelled the ridiculous urge to cover the telltale throbbing with her fingers.

She became aware of warmth leaping from his body to hers as their glances merged together, and she felt an unfamiliar sense of security stealing over her. She had never felt this way before. His eyes seemed to be melting the coldness within her, as if he were attempting to discover the essence of her very being.

"There can be pleasure in lovemaking, Laura," he whispered. "Let me show you."

His eyes devoured her mouth as his head lowered slowly toward his goal. Warm breath fanned her lips, and she trembled uncontrollably.

"N-no, please . . . "

43

She thought her plea unspoken, until she felt the stiffening of the arms holding her.

"Don't cry, honey," he muttered, releasing her and getting to his feet. "We'll take it one step at a time, all right?"

Mutely she nodded, incapable of making even the smallest remark. She watched as he walked to the door, his long legs making nonsense of the distance. He moved with surefooted grace for such a big man, his body utterly responsive to the control he exerted. As the door closed behind him, even the memory of his smile could do nothing to dispel the chill replacing the momentary warmth she had felt in his arms.

As she paced the room, she remembered his parting words. "We'll take it one step at a time . . . one step at a time." She wouldn't see him again; she couldn't. One step would lead to another, and still another . . . and before long it wouldn't be only his own life he controlled, but also hers!

3

H ow was your weekend, Laura?'' Somehow managing a forced laugh, Laura headed for the large, perpetually untidy desk situated in front of her office. Josie, a buxom gray-haired woman of indeterminate age, greeted her with her usual sour-faced grin.

"Exciting as usual, Josie. Saturday I cleaned house, Sunday did my laundry, and so on.''

"Ahhh . . . what it is to be young," Josie sighed, rolling her eyes expressively. Grimacing, Laura told Josie she felt about eighty that morning, which indeed she did. She hadn't slept well since Jace's visit, and last night was no exception. She couldn't seem to control her thoughts of him, and was furious with herself for her weakness.

"Oh, thanks, Josie." Gratefully accepting the proffered coffee, she cupped the steaming mug in her hands. "What would I do without you?"

"Humph! I'll be around for a long time yet, so don't count your chickens. If this morning's phone call is anything to go by, you're going to have worries aplenty.''

With a groan, Laura perched on the edge of Josie's desk. "Tell me the worst," she sighed.

"Mrs. Cabral called. It seems young Miguel didn't come home last night. He's been running around with a pretty rough crowd over the last couple of months, and I gather Maria's at her wits' end."

"That doesn't sound at all like Miguel." She frowned, shaken by the seriousness in Josie's voice. Miguel had been only twelve when his father died of a heart attack, leaving his family nearly destitute, she remembered. Such a brave little guy, the oldest of six children, and determined to take over the responsibilities of the man of the house.

Laura unlocked the door to her office. "Josie, call Maria and tell her I'll be over at five o'clock, if that's convenient. I'll want Miguel present, if possible."

"Will do," Josie promised. "Oh, by the way. You do remember that you have a nine-o'clock meeting this morning with the representatives from Medicare?"

"Thanks, Josie." She grimaced, turning to enter her office. She quickly hung her coat on the hook set in the wall behind her desk, and moved to unlock the file cabinets. With determination, she closed her mind to everything but the business at hand, soon becoming engrossed in her work.

"Laura, it's eight-fifty," Josie barked, sticking her head around the door.

Finishing her notations in the last folder, Laura sat back with a groan. "Thanks, I'll be leaving in a minute, Josie."

How she survived the next couple of hours, she never knew. Once again the government had issued new price changes, which meant that all her files would have to be updated and the various codes changed. Her hand was numb by the time the meeting was adjourned, her notepad a confusing jumble of figures. Her head felt as if it would burst from the noise level in the stuffy room.

"How did it go?" Josie questioned, following Laura into her office.

Laura threw her notepad on her desk, her face mirroring her frustration.

"Like that, was it? I heard rumors hinting at another increase, and figured that was what this meeting was all about. Here, take these. From the looks of you this morning, you need them," she grunted, holding two aspirin in the palm of her hand.

"Josie, you're priceless!" Laura laughed.

Much to Josie's disgust, Laura worked through her lunch hour, updating the files on her desk with the new changes. She was half an hour early for her appointment with the Cabral family, but Maria was already waiting for her.

After greeting a rather shamefaced Miguel, she sat down to listen. Miguel was frustrated, and rightly so, she thought sympathetically. It must be terribly difficult to be expected to perform like any other teenager in school while watching your mother age before your eyes from overwork. He had a part-time job after his last class of the day, but the money he brought home was woefully little.

"Miguel, this is your senior year, isn't it?" Laura knew very well it was, but she wanted the chance to study Miguel before offering any suggestions.

At his affirmative nod, she leaned forward in her chair. "Have you considered taking the high-school equivalency examination?"

Miguel's eyes lit up, and she sat back with relief. He wasn't trying to pull the wool over her eyes, his expression told her that. For Maria's benefit, she went on to explain about the GED test, which would enable Miguel to receive his diploma without delay.

Miguel began an excited discussion in Spanish with Maria, and as Laura watched them, she was filled with a familiar sense of defeat. Miguel was intelligent, but university was out of the question. Even if he received a scholarship, he wouldn't be able to accept. His family needed his help, and he wouldn't sacrifice them for a moment longer than necessary, even if it meant better lives for them all eventually.

The week was a long one, and by Friday she thought she would scream if faced with another problem. She hadn't slept well the last few nights, and it showed. She had been relieved to get home, determined to spend the evening quietly with a book.

The sound of the front door opening interrupted the exhausted reverie she had fallen into in front of her dressing-table mirror. With a last disparaging glance, which took in faint shadows under her eyes and a pinched look about her mouth, she went to greet Cheryl.

"Go get ready to paint the town, Laura," Cheryl demanded, not bothering with a greeting. "No, don't argue. Frank and I are taking you out for your birthday."

"But—"

"No buts," she laughed pushing Laura through the hallway. "We're going to gorge ourselves on Italian food. I hope you're hungry."

Caught up in Cheryl's excitement, Laura felt her fatigue disappear as if by magic. Hurrying through a bath, she returned to her bedroom wrapped in a large fluffy towel. At the sight of the dress laid out on the bed, she stopped and stared. With shaking fingers she reached out and caressed the lovely material.

"Do you like it?" Cheryl stood framed in the doorway, her face wearing a worried frown. "It's a birthday present from Frank and me."

"Like it? Oh, Cheryl, it's marvelous," she breathed, having a great deal of difficulty speaking past the lump in her throat. "I . . . I don't know what to say."

Cheryl walked over and hugged her. "Then don't say anything, silly. I can't wait to see Frank's face when he sees you. You'll knock his eyes out!"

The dress fit to perfection, and she could hardly believe the reflection in the mirror was her own. The style was deceptively simple, but the overall effect was stunning. Of bronze silk, it hugged every curve of her body before falling in graceful folds to ankle length. A deep side split created freedom of movement, and she loved the rustling whisper of sound as she walked.

Hearing Frank's voice in the other room, she bit her lower lip in indecision. It seemed almost a sacrilege to wear her hair in its usual style, and with a burst of defiance she released the long curling tresses from confinement. The difference in her appearance was astounding. Long, shimmering strands caressed the pearly bareness of her shoulders and back, rippling with hidden fire to her waist. She felt free suddenly, like a different woman.

"Well, do you approve?" Irrepressible mirth bubbled from her slightly parted lips as she pivoted, arms raised, hair whirling wildly with her movements.

"God!"

Laura froze as a shadow detached itself from in front of the living-room window and walked slowly toward her.

She must have imagined the sound of that strangled exclamation, she thought. As he approached, he seemed almost insultingly impervious to her appearance.

"Jace, I didn't realize you were here," she said, a nervous smile replacing her earlier spontaneity.

"Apparently not," he remarked, his eyes inspecting her leisurely. "I didn't think all of this was for my benefit."

Blushing, she turned to Cheryl. "Why didn't you let me know Jace was here?"

"He only arrived a couple of minutes ago, and I was afraid you'd lock yourself in your room, if you want the truth." Cheryl's chin was tilted at its most defiant angle, while her eyes moved from Laura to Jace with open speculation.

"You have been known to avoid me in the past, Laura."

At the mocking inflection in Jace's voice, she gasped indignantly. Cheryl and Frank exchanged speaking looks, and as she glanced at their amused faces, her sense of humor got the better of her. As she met Jace's blandly innocent expression, she couldn't control her laughter any longer. His rumbling mirth blended with hers, increasing in volume as they turned to Cheryl and Frank, who were looking at the two of them with good-humored indulgence.

Shared laughter set the tone for the rest of the evening. Laura learned that Jace, who had earlier questioned her parents about the exact date of her birthday, had dropped by with the intention of taking her to celebrate if she were free. As soon as the words were out of his mouth, he was being invited by Frank to join their party, and Laura felt too absurdly happy to offer any objections.

Laura felt like a fairy princess as they traveled into San

Francisco, and no wonder. Jace's blue Mercedes was the essence of sleek luxury, and she glanced often at the strong, capable hands guiding its movements.

The restaurant was in North Beach, the center of the city's Italian community. Since Jace informed them that parking might be hard to come by, they left the Mercedes on the outskirts of the city, taking the Taylor and Bay cable car. Using the excuse that there wasn't enough room, Frank pulled Cheryl onto his lap, sending an encouraging grin in Jace's direction. Before Laura could do more than gasp, Jace had scooped her into his arms and deposited her firmly in position.

"Frank," Cheryl hissed. "Will you stop that!"

"Shush, woman!"

There was a muffled giggle from Cheryl, followed by an evocative silence, and Laura's face flamed in embarrassment. Jace's hand seemed to burn her naked back, while her own fingers tingled where they clutched his neck.

She knew he wasn't fooled by her pretended interest in the scenery. Her breathing was quick, becoming even more shallow when his thumb began a maddening caress upon her smooth skin.

"Does that bother you?" He accompanied his question with a backward inclination of his head. It took her a few seconds to realize he meant Cheryl and Frank.

"It shouldn't, you know. All the world loves a lover, and those two are obviously very much in love."

She didn't know which was worse, his warm breath fanning her ear as he spoke, or his fingers gliding gently over her shoulder to the base of her neck. She squirmed uncomfortably, longing for the interminable ride to be over.

Finally they reached their destination, a three-block walk from North Beach. As the cable car groaned to a stop, she was pushed even closer to Jace, and she froze when he buried his mouth in her hair, both arms moving to hold her fiercely for endless seconds.

"Thank God," he muttered. "If you'd wriggled just once more, I wouldn't have been responsible for my actions."

She managed to regain her composure during the short walk to Di Grande, where they dined upon some of the most delicious Italian food she had ever tasted. Afterward they strolled along the streets, where every shop seemed to cater to gourmet tastes. They passed bakeries, pastry shops, delicatessens, and kitchen specialty stores, until finally Laura was overwhelmed by the variety of sights and smells.

The return ride on the cable car was far more comfortable than the earlier trip had been, at least that was what Laura told herself. It was practically empty, and Frank and Jace, deep in a conversation carried over from dinner, sat together. She didn't know who was the quieter, she or Cheryl.

As Jace drove back across the bridge, she found his attitude puzzling. "Is something the matter, Jace?"

She relaxed when he slanted a sudden smile in her direction. She hadn't been aware of how tense she had become with the increasing silence in the car. Cheryl was half-asleep, snuggled comfortably against Frank, so there'd be no help from that direction.

"I'm sorry, honey. Late nights catching up on me, I guess."

An intense flash of jealousy took her by surprise. She wondered who had shared those late nights with Jace, and although she had no right, she felt shaken with anger.

"Oh?" Her face was carefully controlled as she looked at him, or so she thought. She wanted to crawl into a hole and die when he casually mentioned jet lag.

"Y-you've been traveling?"

"Mmmm, I just got back from the Birmingham foundry this afternoon, in time for a meeting with your father and several government representatives. I'm sorry I'm being such a wet blanket on your birthday."

"Birthday!" she exploded. "You should be home in bed, not out celebrating my birthday!"

"A cold bed doesn't hold much appeal!"

Laura was silenced by the barely disguised harshness in his voice, as well as by the swiftly penetrating look he sent in her direction. She was relieved when Frank leaned forward to talk to Jace. It gave her the time she needed to regain her composure. The implication in his words had been clear, even though she couldn't take exception to the context. She didn't know whether to be angry or flattered. Her latter thought startled her. Why should she be flattered by the idea that Jace blamed her for the coldness of his bed? If he didn't like it, he could just buy himself an electric blanket. He was fully aware of her feelings toward him.

She had been so wrapped up in her thoughts, she hadn't paid much attention to her surroundings.

"Where are we?"

"Frank's apartment," he replied. "He asked me to drop him off."

"But his car's at our place!"

Laura knew she sounded slightly panicky, and Jace's expression reflected knowing amusement. When she turned toward the backseat to question Frank, the words froze in her throat as he lifted a sleeping Cheryl into his arms.

"Thanks, Jace," Frank whispered. "We'll catch the bus later. I'll need my car in the morning."

"Don't thank me yet, Frank," he chuckled. "You're going to be in for it when she wakes up."

Far from worried, Frank grinned, expressing a world of confidence as he glanced tenderly down at the sleeping girl in his arms. "Don't I know it. If that wedding date doesn't hurry up and get here, I'm going to die of frustration!"

Laura's nerves were stretched to the breaking point by the time they finally parked in front of her apartment. She had no intention of asking him in for coffee, but one look at the exhaustion whitening his features made her change her mind.

As they entered the darkened apartment, the uneasy feeling that she'd made a mistake in asking him in only increased, but it was too late to worry about that now. The way he looked, he needed something to keep him awake. It would be just like him to fall asleep at the wheel and end up killing himself, she thought. She wasn't going to have his death on her conscience because of something as trivial as a cup of coffee.

Jace had wandered into the living room as soon as they arrived, and even though she strained her ears, she couldn't hear any sounds emanating from that direction. Waiting for the coffee to finish perking, she drummed her fingers on the tile sink. She was behaving irrationally, but she couldn't seem to stop it. Part of her wanted him as far away from her as possible, while another part couldn't stand the idea of being alone.

She dispensed with a tray. The last thing she wanted was sleeplessness, and she ought to be able to manage carrying a single mug without mishap—at least she hoped so. A horrible vision of her tripping and splattering Jace with coffee made her want to giggle.

Setting the mug on the coffee table, Laura turned to speak to Jace, but the words were never uttered. She stared at him in consternation. He was stretched out on the divan, one leather-shod foot on the gold carpeting, while the other dangled over the edge. Tan slacks molded powerful thighs snugly, and Laura flushed as she realized the fascinated direction of her inspection. Raising her head nervously, she was relieved to find his eyes still closed.

Standing immobile, she felt confident enough to inspect his face, noticing the length of his thick lashes with a feeling of surprise. They were quite beautiful, and certainly didn't belong on a face of such strength and square-jawed obstinacy. Her gaze traveled to his throat in swift inspection, and down to where a cream silk shirt stretched over a muscular chest and forearms.

"Jace," she whispered. Then, more loudly, "Jace, wake up!"

Not by the flicker of an eyelid did he show that her words had reached him, and with an exasperated sigh she approached his reclining figure. A fleeting tenderness warmed her as she stood over him. He looked vulnerable with his features softened in sleep. She gave in to the irresistible compulsion to touch him, her hand trembling as it came into contact with the heat emanating from his silk-clad arm. The divan was low, and she could feel her heart pounding thunderously as she bent to complete the movement, wondering why the sound of her heartbeat alone wasn't enough to wake him.

"J-Jace, your coffee's ready." She accompanied her words with a tightening shake of her fingers, and was relieved when his eyes opened and a lazy smile curved his mouth.

All at once she was trapped within a silver web, unable to move away from the power he exerted over her. Since their first meeting, he had caused her to experience a gamut of unfamiliar emotions, until now she was rendered helpless by her own vulnerability.

Jace's eyes widened, seeking and finding an answering chord to his own growing excitement in her unguarded expression. Her name on his lips was a sigh which struck an answering spark of longing in her breast, and she shook with the force of her response.

Laura was never able to remember how she came to be lying beside him, wedged between the back of the divan and his body. A feeling of total unreality made her pliant in his arms, arms which curved her to his body as if she were meant to be there. Her eyes, wide pools of torment, looked into his with the desperation of a trapped animal, and his hand was gentle against her heated cheek, his thumb moving caressingly against her closed lips.

"Don't tremble so, honey," he murmured, closing each eyelid with his mouth. "I'm not going to hurt you."

She was unprepared when his lips replaced his probing thumb. True to his word, his kiss began as a softly tentative exploration, and she was too stunned by the swift shaft of white-hot pleasure to deny him her response. She could feel his muscles tensing when her mouth opened beneath his. With a sense of wonder, she realized he was trembling every bit as much as she was. Then, without warning, his control snapped, and with a groan he deepened the pressure of his lips on hers. His tongue began a delicate foray into the moist receptiveness of her mouth, and he gasped in arousal when she involuntarily arched against him.

A sudden shiver of pleasure caused her to dig her heels into the soft velvet of the divan. Looking toward the source, she saw Jace's head bent to her breast, his tongue circling the dampened silk of her dress in an erotic pattern. To her disgust, she became aware of the full extent of her body's betrayal, as a hardened nipple strained upward in unmistakable delight.

At the sight, the cold, analytical part of her brain began functioning once again, but to her despair it wasn't enough to curb her treacherous responses. His hand, moving sensuously down her back until it cupped softly rounded flesh, began pushing her against his aroused hardness. Warning lights flashed in her brain, and she began to struggle. Anguished by her abrupt awakening to a passion she hadn't known she could feel, she became frightened by the evocatively rhythmic thrusting of his hips. Her eyes dilated with shamed awareness as her body, seemingly of its own accord, rose to meet the demand of his. Unable to believe herself capable of such abandonment, she felt her control finally snap, and sobs shook her unmercifully.

"Laura, for God's sake, stop it!"

Her entire body shuddered under the onslaught of her emotions.

With a muffled curse, Jace moved away from her. His head was bent as he attempted to quiet his breathing, and she saw the tremor in his hands as they raked his hair back from his damp forehead. Jace kept his head averted, and she knew the action was deliberate. A new emotion, that of guilt, was making itself felt, and her insides churned with remorse. She was totally to blame for this situation, but the admission didn't make it any easier to bear. Knowing he had only responded to the newly burgeoning hunger inside of her, she couldn't condemn him for the savagery of his next remark.

"There's a name for women like you!"

Laura gasped, recoiling as if from a blow. His eyes were like ice, coldly furious. She wanted to scream against a pain so intense she was nearly maddened by it.

"J-Jace, please . . ."

The word he hurled at her was shockingly direct, and her eyes widened in horrified disbelief as she was suddenly seized in a punishing grip. "Damn you, do I look like a boy, used to being teased until I'm nearly out of my mind, and then denied at the last moment? You're a grown woman, not some teenager using virginity as an escape. Or are you the type who enjoys seeing a man squirm?"

"I . . ." she said, her mouth shaking uncontrollably as she fought back more tears. "I didn't mean this to happen, I s-swear I didn't. I haven't any excuse f-for acting the way I did. I'm not in the habit of . . . of teasing men for the fun of it, no matter what you think!"

He stood in front of her, his eyes on her bent head as he slowly buttoned his shirt.

"Then what went wrong, Laura? Is it personal? Did I do something you didn't like?"

The gentleness in his voice was her undoing. With a wretchedness too intense to be borne, she covered her face with her hands. "Jace, I . . . I'm sorry. I just didn't know it was possible for me to react like that," she whispered, still unable to believe the extent of her emotions. "My husband made me think I was useless where sex was concerned, and I believed him. He used to mock me because I wouldn't respond to him, but I couldn't . . . I couldn't!"

"Look at me, Laura!"

Like a child expecting further punishment, she obeyed the harsh command. She cringed as his hand came up to smooth the hair from her face, and his eyes flickered in momentary pain.

"You don't have to be frightened of me, honey. I won't hurt you, or demand more than you can give—that I promise you. We'll take it slowly. You need time to absorb the fact that you're truly a woman in the fullest sense, and I intend to give it to you."

With a muffled exclamation he pulled her up into his arms, murmuring words of remorse until he felt her relaxing. Holding her away from the warmth of his body, he smiled, while his thumb gently explored the softness of her cheek.

Her eyes were wide as she stared into his, held by a compassion and understanding she was almost afraid to believe in . . . didn't want to believe in. To believe would be to fall into another trap, only this time it would be Jace she would have to put her trust in. The thought was terrifying, and her expression darkened with the fear of commitment. Phillip had hurt her pride—she realized that now; but Jace—he could destroy her!

With a pathetic attempt at dignity, she moved away from him, smoothing her clothes with deadly calmness.

"I want you to leave now," she said tonelessly, and he could see the sudden rejection in her eyes.

"Laura . . ."

"I want you to leave . . . *now!*"

Even though she knew he would do as she asked, the sound of the door closing behind him startled her, and she glanced at the wooden surface with suddenly wild eyes. Her restraint snapped, and she sank to her knees in an agony of pain.

By the end of a month, Laura was still no nearer to forgetting Jace than she had been throughout that long, miserable night she had spent after her birthday celebration. For the first couple of weeks, Jace called her continually, but she refused to speak to him. Obviously he had gotten the message, because the calls abruptly stopped. Illogically, instead of feeling relieved, she felt betrayed . . . and she hated herself as day followed day.

"Laura, what in the world are you doing?"

Straightening her aching back from its crouched position on the kitchen floor, she turned to face an indignant Cheryl.

"I thought I'd clean the grout on the tiles," she replied. "What are you doing back so early? I thought you were spending the day with Frank."

"I was, but there was a freeway pile-up on the Nimitz, and the hospital called for him just as we were ready to leave."

"What rotten luck." Getting to her feet, Laura laid the bristled cleaning brush on the kitchen counter. "I know you were looking forward to shopping for your trousseau."

"Mmmm, but it doesn't really matter. Frank's next to useless when it comes to shopping, unless I'm modeling bikinis. That's the only thing that holds his interest for very long." Cheryl laughed, taking a glass from the cupboard and going to the refrigerator.

Drinking her milk with relish, she suddenly turned to Laura, her eyes beginning to sparkle with animation. "Why don't you and I go?"

"Oh, Cheryl," she protested, waving her hand vaguely toward the floor. "There's so much to do here, and I'm not really in the mood."

With a sense of guilt, Laura realized that it had been a long time since she and Cheryl had gone anywhere together, either alone or in company. Not since the night . . . "I . . . I'm sorry, Cheryl. I've been rotten company these last few weeks, haven't I?"

"Do you expect me to deny it, Laura?"

"No, but I—"

"Look, I'm your friend, you don't owe me any explanations," Cheryl interrupted, facing Laura with her hands on her hips and her chin tilted belligerently. "I know perfectly well what your problem is, but you're not going to solve it by working yourself to death. You've spent your weekends shut up in this apartment, cleaning as if your life depended on it, and according to Josie, you aren't much better off at work."

"Josie's an old fusspot," Laura mumbled, running a tired hand through her tumbled hair.

"She's as worried about you as I am," Cheryl retorted. The disgusted expression contorting her face caused Laura to flush with embarrassed awareness. Glancing down at the grubby jeans and old gray flannel shirt which was a relic of her teens, she could imagine how she looked to her friend.

A small, slim-fingered hand clutched her arm, and

Laura looked at it in surprise. She had almost completely forgotten Cheryl's presence, lost as she had been in self-absorption. With bitterness she realized that this preoccupation with herself was turning her into a stranger, one she didn't like very much. In her case, the old saying "misery loves company" was erroneous. All her misery was locked deeply inside, and she was shutting out the people who cared for her as a result.

"What's wrong with me?"

Briskly Cheryl walked across the floor, her wooden clogs clumping against the tile. Pouring a cup of coffee for Laura and another for herself, she returned.

"Don't *you* know what's wrong?" Cheryl studied the dark liquid in her cup intently, avoiding Laura's eyes. "You know, a good way to get over a man is simply to find another," she advised.

"No!" Laura's repudiation of Cheryl's suggestion was swift and vehement, and Cheryl's eyes widened in satisfaction.

"It's Jace," she cried, a smile curving her lips. "You're in love with him!"

"Don't talk like a fool," Laura said, her mouth twisting angrily. "I want nothing to do with Jace Matthews, not now or ever!"

Cheryl was quick to notice that although Laura denied wanting anything to do with Jace, she didn't deny that she loved him. Studying Laura's sullen expression, Cheryl hid a smile, saying only, "I do believe there's hope for you yet!"

As if attempting to allay Laura's suspicions, Cheryl began chattering unconcernedly, describing the garments she was planning to buy for her trousseau. In spite of herself, Laura's interest was caught, and she replied to Cheryl's conversational gambit with growing enthusiasm.

From that point on, Laura thought later, she was putty in her friend's hands. Before she knew it, she had showered and changed into a blue cowl-necked knit dress. Its clinging folds made her recent weight loss more apparent, but it would have to do, she decided.

As they drove across the Bay Bridge linking the Oakland Bay Area with San Francisco, she began to relax. The day was bright and crystal clear, and the skyline of San Francisco looked magnificent in the distance. The water changed from blue to green, depending upon its depth and the reflection of light on its choppy surfaces. Rolling down the window until the cool breeze played against her face, she breathed the salty tang of the ocean with a feeling of pleasurable anticipation. It seemed forever since she had really looked forward to anything, and now she couldn't help being glad at Cheryl's insistence.

Leaving the car in a four-story underground parking garage, she was surprised to find she was enjoying herself. Union Square, with its beautiful lawns and formal gardens in the heart of downtown San Francisco, encouraged a leisurely exploration of the exclusive dress salons and marvelous boutiques. Though sunshine poured from cloudless blue skies overhead, the crisp breezes off the bay made a coat a necessity. After two days of almost incessant rain, the expression on the faces of shoppers and tourists reflected delight in what amounted to a perfect San Francisco day.

By the time they stopped for lunch, Laura was famished. This told her as clearly as anything that she was beginning to emerge from the vacuum she had created around herself during the past few weeks. Her appetite lately had been nonexistent, and she was pleased to find herself anticipating a meal with pleasure again.

After giving her order, she glanced around while Cheryl talked with their waitress. The walls were adorned with pictures from the movie *Casablanca*, from which the restaurant derived its name. Sitting amid a mellow blend of palm trees, Oriental rugs and ceiling fans, she found herself responding to the romantic atmosphere with sadness.

This was the kind of place she could imagine Jace bringing her to, and the thought brought wrenching unhappiness in its wake. No matter how many times she told herself she had been right to sever their relationship, she couldn't help wondering when she would begin to believe it.

She had been staring at the crystal water decanter on the table steadily for the last several minutes. Raised spirals dipped and circled each other in a pleasantly smooth pattern, and she wondered why her life couldn't be like that. A feeling of injustice flowed through her, and she had to fight an insane urge to grip the decanter and fling it across the room.

During those introspective moments, Laura finally faced the truth about herself, and she didn't like what she saw. She felt awful—not because she had severed her relationship with Jace, but because she had been too afraid to establish one. Inner pride balked at the thought of being a coward, but that's exactly what she was, she realized. She wasn't fleeing from Jace, but from herself.

By the time they left the restaurant, Laura's spirits were higher than they'd been for weeks. The thought of Jace, so long suppressed, no longer had the power to hurt her. The next time he calls, she vowed silently, I'll let him know what a fool I've been.

It didn't take long for her friends at work to notice the change in Laura. After leaving the restaurant with Cheryl, she had indulged in her own orgy of shopping, and to say that the result left her co-workers gasping was minimizing the effect she made on Monday morning. Instead of one of the tailored suits she normally appeared in for work, she was arrayed in a softly clinging jersey shift in a shade between cinnamon and bronze, her burnished hair artfully arranged in a softly upswept style.

It wasn't only her appearance which was remarked on whenever she passed. Never very outgoing, Laura had kept a lot to herself in the past, but she was determined to change that. She smiled and laughed and joked, and as the days passed, it became easier and more natural. For the first time in her life she felt she was liked as well as admired from a distance, and the knowledge soothed the bewildered hurt she was feeling at Jace's continued silence.

She would be glad when this week was finally over, she mused tiredly as she waited for the elevator at the end of the day. Cheryl had rushed into her office earlier, to let her know they were having company for dinner. Although she hadn't said anything at the time, the last thing Laura wanted was an apartment full of people. Of course, even if she had had any objections, she wouldn't have had much time to voice them. Almost before she could open her mouth, Cheryl hurried off, explaining that Frank was double-parked on the busy street below.

"Good evening, Miss Spencer."

Laura jumped, turning to face Bert, one of the older night watchmen who guarded the building. Her color rose slightly, and he looked at her fondly.

"You'd better be heading home now; it looks like you've been working too hard again," he advised, his face creased with fatherly concern. "It's almost seven. A little late, even for you."

"Is it seven o'clock already?" As she spoke, she looked at the gold-bracelet band of her watch with consternation. "You know how I get carried away, Bert. Heavens, I'll have to rush. Cheryl's going to kill me if I'm late for dinner!"

"Good night, Miss Spencer," he called after her departing figure.

4

~~~~~~~~~

Letting herself into her apartment with lagging footsteps, Laura turned to close the door while rubbing the back of her neck in an attempt to ease the tension.

"Laura, I thought I heard you come in."

"Hi, how's everything going?" Laura asked, walking toward her bedroom with Cheryl following. "Just let me grab a quick shower and I'll help you finish. Who's coming tonight, anyway?"

Cheryl plopped down on the end of Laura's bed with a relieved groan. "Everything's finished, so don't hurry. I hadn't planned dinner until eight-thirty anyway. You've got plenty of time."

With these words Cheryl gave Laura an encouraging grin before jumping nervously to her feet. "I'd better check the roast," she muttered, hurrying from the room.

"Where's the fire?" Laura called after her, chuckling when Cheryl paused long enough to aim a speaking glance in her direction.

Laura's shower wasn't the bath she wanted, but it did

67

help her to feel slightly more human. Dressing in an apricot sheath, which should have clashed horribly with her hair but didn't, she felt satisfied with her appearance. The dress, one of her recent purchases, was both comfortable and elegant, and she congratulated herself on forgoing her uneasy doubts regarding the color, and buying it anyway.

Entering the kitchen, she noticed the perfection of the dining table as she passed. Fine white china was laid regally on Cheryl's best lace tablecloth, and a centerpiece of deep red roses in a crystal vase added a dramatic touch of color to the otherwise white table setting.

"Who are we expecting, the President?" Laura spoke to Cheryl's back as she crossed the room and got a water glass from the cupboard. She didn't hear Cheryl's mumbled reply, the sound being drowned out by the running tap water.

"Who?" she asked, shutting off the water and leaning against the sink, a sense of forboding stealing over her as she inspected Cheryl's averted face.

"Frank and I've invited Jace for dinner."

"Cheryl, how could you?" Laura stammered, a look of dawning horror crossing her features. "He'll think I planned all of this!"

"Now, calm down," Cheryl soothed, removing her apron and laying it beside Laura before facing her. "I made it perfectly clear to him that the idea wasn't yours, so don't worry about it. The only question he asked was whether you'd be here, and when I said you would, he accepted. If he didn't want to see you again, he would have refused the invitation, wouldn't he?"

"If he wanted to see me again," Laura retorted, "he would have done something about it before now."

"Do you mean he should have called you, only to be told you wouldn't speak with him? No, better yet, he should have come around and had the door slammed in his face!"

"Cheryl, that's not fair," Laura said, hurt by her friend's sarcasm. "You know I wouldn't—"

"I know that, and you know that, but Jace doesn't. The man has his pride, Laura."

The sound of the doorbell interrupted their altercation, and Laura felt a strong urge to flee. Her mouth was dry, and her heart pounded frantically against her rib cage. Her panic didn't decrease when Cheryl pushed her toward the door.

"Go answer it, Laura. I've got to slice the roast."

Moistening her lips with the tip of her tongue, she blindly obeyed Cheryl's orders. Standing briefly in the brightly lit hallway, she swallowed with difficulty, desperately trying to gain her composure. The thought of Jace standing only a few feet away sent sharp tingles of awareness rippling through her, and she didn't know how to greet him, panicky at the idea of opening the door and just standing before him like a tongue-tied teenager.

When she finally found the courage to release the latch, Jace was greeted by a beautifully poised individual devoid of warmth.

"Hello, Laura!"

Just the sound of his voice was enough to send a tingle down her spine, and as if in a nightmare, she heard herself mumble inanely. Their eyes seemed to be locked together, as if he were attempting to see into her soul, she thought. Apparently he was satisfied with his inspection, because a slow smile curved his mouth as he walked toward her.

Laura closed the door automatically, unable to tear her gaze from his firm, mobile mouth. Once again she moistened her lips, just the tip of her pink tongue caressing their dryness, and at a sudden exclamation from Jace, she turned startled eyes upward. Before she could protest, he drew her toward him, his hands hard upon her arched back.

"I've missed you like hell, honey," he murmured, and as his mouth lowered to hers, all rational thought left her. For long moments only the feeling of his kiss registered, his head moving back and forth slowly in an evocative rhythm. Without conscious volition her mouth softened and opened under his, and she felt him tremble with a suppressed need matching her own as their breath mingled. She clutched his upper arms for support, finding pleasure in the feel of rough cloth beneath her palms. His sport coat was of blue-and-green tweed, firmly molding his superb figure, and she shocked herself by the urge, so strong as to be almost unbearable, to unbutton that jacket and slide her hands closer to his skin.

"Mmmm, that was worth waiting for," he murmured at last, his breath warm against her temple.

A feeling of rage rippled through her, and she pushed herself out of his arms. The nerve of him, to walk in here as if she were a parcel stamped and ready for delivery!

"If you were so eager to see me again, you have a funny way of showing it," she snapped. "I don't know why you kissed me, because obviously I leave you cold, or you would have been around before now. And another thing, I hadn't the least idea, until a few minutes ago, that you were even coming. If I'd known, I'd have eaten out."

"I know, that's why I told Cheryl to keep quiet," he confessed, a rueful grin slanting his mouth. "And as for you leaving me cold, you must be out of your mind!"

As he spoke, he reached for her again, but she evaded his hands, her face mutinous. "So this was a conspiracy," she hissed through clenched teeth. "I should have known!"

"Right the first time," he admitted unrepentantly, following her swiftly moving body into the dining room as she headed for the kitchen. "I figured you'd had enough time to come to your senses."

Turning on him, she clenched her fists at her sides impotently. "What do you mean, until I had time to come to *my* senses? You're the one who needs his head examined. Don't get the idea I've been sitting around here waiting for you to call, you inconsiderate, pigheaded—"

Throwing his head back, Jace roared with laughter, reaching out and grabbing her as she furiously turned to leave. With one finger beneath her chin, he forced her eyes to his, and his laughter ended abruptly as he saw her eyes clouded with misery.

"I meant that I stayed away deliberately, giving you the time to admit you want me as much as I want you."

"Well, I won't," she gulped, shivering as a hard hand caressed her neck and the curve of her jaw.

"Won't what?" His whispered question was accompanied by a finger lightly tracing the stubborn curve of her mouth.

"Won't admit I want you," she gasped, pulling away from his grasp with trembling limbs.

71

"I'll take that to mean you do want me, but you just won't admit it," he chuckled, his eyes surveying her body slowly, his gaze burning through her clothes.

Stunned for letting herself fall into his trap, she blushed when she realized what she had admitted by her unguarded words. Stammering, she attempted to refute his allegations, but suddenly the humor of the situation struck her, and she began laughing. "You're impossible, do you know that?"

Bending, he kissed the tip of her tilted nose. "Is that why you melt against me whenever I hold you in my arms?"

Stumbling into the kitchen, Laura avoided Cheryl's amused smile. Frank chose that moment to arrive, for which she was grateful. Helping to carry the food into the dining room, she was conscious of Jace's eyes, but strangely enough, the thought of him watching her wasn't annoying. He found her attractive, and she was pleased by the knowledge.

She studied him as he conversed with Frank, enjoying the deep timbre of his voice, the expressions fleetingly crossing his mobile face. Several times he caught her looking at him, and he would smile at her with a tenderness which was almost her undoing.

It was with a sense of resentment that she turned to answer a question from Cheryl, tearing her gaze from Jace with effort. At Cheryl's mocking expression she could feel heat flooding her face. She was being as obvious as a moonstruck teenager, she thought in disgust. What in the world was there about the man that seemed to wrap her in a somnolent aura whenever he was present? She hated the hold he had over her, yet she was all too willing to allow herself to be drawn deeper into his web. Soon she would have no will of her own, she warned herself.

"Why don't we have coffee in the living room?" Cheryl questioned brightly, jumping to her feet and beginning to clear the table.

"Good idea, honey." Frank grinned. "I'll light the fire and do a little furniture arranging."

"Franklin Simmons, you behave yourself," Cheryl warned, her own grin matching Frank's suggestive leer.

"Now, we want to give Jace and Laura a little privacy, don't we?"

"We don't need any privacy, thank you all the same, Frank," Laura insisted, embarrassed nervousness making it impossible to meet Frank's twinkling eyes.

"I'll help you, Frank," Jace laughed, sending a wink in Frank's direction. "I know just how I want things arranged. Laura may not want any privacy, but I certainly do."

With a disdainful toss of her head, Laura stormed into the kitchen, nearly running over Cheryl in the process. After rinsing the plates and cutlery and placing them in the dishwasher, she and Cheryl arranged the tray for coffee.

"Cheryl, you and Frank aren't . . . well, you aren't planning to leave, are you?"

Frowning curiously, Cheryl placed the cups on the tray while Laura fiddled with the creamer. "No, of course not," she replied. "Why do you ask?"

Suddenly the reason for Laura's anxiety became apparent to Cheryl, and she burst into peals of laughter. "You don't have to worry. We aren't planning on leaving you alone," she choked, patting Laura on the shoulder reassuringly.

"Well, don't," Laura muttered, her face flushed and her eyes mutinous. "I don't want to give Jace any ideas."

Carrying the tray, Cheryl chuckled and murmured over her shoulder, "No one will have to give that man any ideas where you're concerned, Laura. Not the way he's been eating you with his eyes all evening."

The sound of masculine laughter greeted them as they stepped down into the living room, and as the reason for their mirth became apparent, all of Laura's worst fears were realized. Softly seductive shadows were flickering on the walls from the fire, and the subdued strains of her favorite jazz record could be heard teasing the air. The divan sectional had been turned and separated, the cushions placed on the floor in front of the fire, the table between them. Frank and Jace were standing, one on each side, with almost identical gleams in their eyes.

"Come over here, Laura," Jace demanded softly. "Cheryl . . . let me take that tray. Why don't you go sit over there, and let Frank and me wait on the two of you for a change?"

Cheryl allowed Jace to relieve her of her burden, meeting his gaze and arching her eyebrow in a wry quirk. "From the looks of this, you two have the entertainment all planned."

Laura felt foolish standing in the middle of the room, and although she knew she'd regret it, she allowed herself to be seated among the cushions. She was making too much of the whole situation, anyway. Even though they couldn't see, or be seen, there wasn't much Jace could accomplish, with Cheryl and Frank just a few feet away!

Within moments Laura knew how wrong her supposition had been. Jace removed his jacket, and after draping it over the back of the divan, he slowly unbuttoned his shirt to the third button. The short sleeves showed off his muscular arms to advantage, the sight of his rippling bronze biceps forcing her to look away nervously.

"Is the jazz yours?"

"Wh-what? Oh, yes," she stammered, watching in fascination as he lowered himself beside her. His movements fluid and unusually graceful for such a large man, he stretched his long legs out in front of him and gave a sigh of contentment as he leaned back. What bothered her, though, was the way his arm automatically reached around behind her until she was leaning against the solidness of his chest.

"We seem to enjoy the same music," he whispered, his mouth nuzzling her temple.

Feeling it more sensible, under the circumstances, to agree with him, Laura nodded her head in an affirmative. She was congratulating herself on the maneuver, which served a twofold purpose, the main being to dislodge his mouth from her tingling skin, when his next words caused her to gasp.

"Let's see what other pleasures we have in common, hmmm?"

Before she could protest, his other hand cupped her neck, and he turned her face toward his. By the time she felt his mouth on hers, any feeble resistance she might have made was suppressed. A feeling of exquisite arousal exploded in her brain, and she shivered convulsively, feeling his arms tighten around her. She wanted this more than she had ever wanted anything else in her life, and her response was more violent than she had believed possible.

"Do you like this, honey?"

Almost mindless with delight, she didn't know which she was enjoying more, his mouth teasing her ear, or his hand kneading the fullness of her breast. Swallowing with difficulty, she tried to tell him how he was making her feel, but found herself unable to verbalize her thoughts.

Slowly he withdrew his mouth, lifting his head until he could look into her eyes. "I asked you a question."

"I . . . I can't, Jace."

It was all right when her eyes were closed; then she could enjoy the sensations while pretending it was somebody else lying here in a welter of sensual pleasure. But when he looked at her, his eyes burning with a need to match her own, she couldn't pretend anymore.

"Dammit, Laura," he rasped. "Why can't you put it into words?"

"I don't know what you mean," she lied, avoiding his eyes.

With a muffled curse he pulled himself erect, his hands deft as he straightened her dress into proper order. She supposed she should be thankful for his consideration, but all she felt was a burning disappointment. She felt ashamed of her emotions, but she couldn't seem to help them. To herself she was more honest than she had been with Jace just moments before. She wanted him, all right. The fluctuation of her heartbeats would have forced her to face the truth, even if she hadn't had the aching pulsing in her lower limbs to prove it.

"You know what I mean, so don't lie to me," he told her, capturing her trembling chin in his palm and turning her head to face him. "Do you think there's something wrong in admitting you want me?"

"What do you expect me to do, with my friends not

twenty feet away—tear off my clothes for you?" Laura was using anger to combat the languorous desire still coursing through her. She resented Jace's ability to turn off his emotions so quickly, to look composed and relaxed as he reclined against the cushions. Even his eyes showed no trace of the darkening passion she had glimpsed in them only moments before, and she could almost hate him for the impenetrable mask his face now wore.

She turned startled eyes in his direction when he grasped her arm, stopping her from rising to her feet.

"We haven't finished our discussion," he mocked, one corner of his mobile mouth curving upward in a travesty of a smile. "We're just getting to the good part. I believe you wanted to know what I expect from you, hmmm?"

"I couldn't care less!"

"I'll just tell you anyway," he murmured, his thumb moving in a disturbing caress on her arm. "There's only one way with you, Laura . . . and that's brutal honesty. I want you, and I'm not ashamed to admit it, but what I want more than the delight of possessing every inch of you is to hear you admit you want me. I want to be the first with you."

A flicker of pain darkened her eyes, and she lowered her head, a tiny pulse beating frantically in her temple.

"You know you wouldn't be the first."

With gentle fingers he caressed her hair, brushing stray tendrils from her neck. "In all the ways that count, you're as innocent as the day you were born," he whispered, his mouth feathering tender kisses against her dampened forehead. "I don't believe you've ever told a man you want him, either with your mouth or your body. Not only that, but until you've fulfilled yourself as a woman, you're as much a virgin as you were before your marriage. I want to give you that, Laura. I want to teach you what making love really means, and I'm determined you'll enjoy every minute of it!"

Her eyes were troubled as they looked into his. He talked as if her capitulation were a foregone conclusion, and she could once again feel her independence being threatened. If he were to be believed, it would only be a matter of time before she gave him what he asked for, but she couldn't . . . she couldn't!

"What are you thinking?"

"Aren't my thoughts even to be my own?" she rasped, firming her mouth and fighting the attraction she felt for him. "You want more than I can give, Jace."

"You'll be gaining far more than I'll take, Laura. When will you realize that?"

"I only need myself," she argued. "The way I see it, you want to take even that from me."

"Yes," he admitted grudgingly, "but you'll never lose the essential essence of yourself, any more than I will. Instead we'll both merge into the other, giving and taking, and changing in the process. I have no guarantees for the future, only hopes. We would both become different people through our loving, honey."

"And can you promise me that I'll like this new woman better, Jace? Can you honestly promise we wouldn't end up like so many other couples, resenting each other for our loss of freedom?"

He shook his head slowly, but his gaze remained locked with hers. "I make no promises, I've already told you that. There's only one thing I'm sure of, and that's the loneliness I saw in you when we first met. I arranged our meeting in a mood of devilment, but I was caught in my own trap, Laura. Curiosity turned to a desire to know more about you. You intrigued me, and I came here with the sole intention of wresting you from my mind. I didn't plan what happened, any more than you did. Do you think I enjoy being dependent on one woman to ease the aching inside me?''

At her look of disbelief he grabbed her shoulders, giving her a tiny shake to emphasize his words. "It's true, damn you. I haven't had a woman since I met you, and I'm getting sick and tired of cold showers. When I left you that night, I felt as if I'd been poleaxed, and believe me, that feeling hasn't subsided one bit," he said, his mouth curving bitterly. "I stopped laughing a long time ago; I no longer find our relationship a bit funny." He dropped his hands in disgust, turning to stare into the leaping flames of the fireplace. "The irony of it is, you don't seem to care how I feel. That's what I can't take."

"I . . . I care," she murmured, knowing how true the words were the moment he turned his incredulous gaze toward her. There was hope in his eyes, but as he reached for her once again, she pulled back. "I . . . I need time, Jace," she pleaded, begging with tear-filled eyes for his understanding, but afraid she wouldn't get it. She relaxed when she saw the harsh line of his mouth curve in a smile, her own eyes tender as she answered with one of her own. "I don't know how to handle this. . . . Please give me time to be sure of my own mind."

"You'll have as much time as you need," he promised, shaking his head in a rueful gesture, "but for God's sake, have a little pity, Laura. I don't know how long I can hold out, honey."

She, too, turned to study the flames, contentment becoming the only reality when his arm enfolded her, drawing her back against his shoulder. For long moments only the crackle of the flames intruded upon her consciousness, and with a sigh she snuggled closer to Jace, her eyelids lowering and becoming heavy with sleep.

She was roused from a somnolent doze when Frank's voice filled the stillness. "Hey, are you two decent over there? I want my coffee."

Before answering, Jace lowered his mouth to hers in a hard kiss which left her weakened desires once more awake and raging.

"Come and get it, Frank." Jace's laughter rippled like an electrical charge over her skin as he turned teasing eyes to hers. "All this woman's doing is sleeping on me, anyway!"

Laura laughed and doubled up her fist, punching him in the chest, and with a mocking leer he lunged at her, tickling her ribs until she begged for mercy.

Looking up, her breath coming in fitful gasps, she was startled to see both Frank and Cheryl grinning down at them from the other side of the couch, and she quickly moved to tug down her dress, which had risen to show a shapely expanse of curving thigh. To her consternation, Jace's hand was there before hers, only he wasn't moving as quickly as she would have, she thought. His palm caressed on its way to her hem, making the simple act one of calculated arousal. The sight of his tanned flesh against the whiteness of her thigh was enough, in itself, to justify the tiny gasp she was unable to suppress, and she noticed the darkening of his eyes as he stared into her own, making her aware of his own pleasure at her reaction.

"Are you two going to take all day?" Cheryl mocked, a giggle bubbling from her lips. "I didn't know it could take so long to pull a dress down."

The burning brand on her leg from Jace's hand had nothing over the burning in her cheeks. With an indignant jerk of her body she rose to her feet, glaring at Jace when he dared to laugh at her discomfiture. "This is all your fault," she hissed, backing away from him instinctively when he stood beside her.

"It'd better be," he growled menacingly, taking a threatening step toward her. "If you acted like this with anyone else, I'd wring your beautiful neck!"

Both Frank and Cheryl were by now howling with laughter, and it was only then that she realized Jace was teasing her, deliberately goading her into acting the fool, she thought. Still, there had been a small element of sincerity in his voice, and she knew he meant his words.

They drank their coffee in front of the fire, and before long Frank stretched tiredly and rose to his feet. "Much as I hate to leave, I've got early call in the morning. See you later, Laura." He smiled, shaking hands with Jace, who was rising to his feet, too. "Jace, I'm guessing I'll see you around more often, which suits me fine."

"Just why would you think that?" Laura retorted, angry at the way things were being taken out of her hands.

Shaking his head in mocking sympathy, Frank laughed. "I don't envy you, man. You've got yourself a wildcat by the tail. Me, I prefer my kittens all soft and purring."

Laura reached behind her and threw a cushion at

Frank's head, and as Jace solemnly nodded an affirmative, she wished she'd thrown two pillows instead of one.

Seeing the warning signs in Laura's face, Cheryl suppressed her own laughter, leading Frank to the door before Laura could throw something heavier at him. Jace, she thought, could take care of himself!

"Come here, kitten."

She was still crouched upon the floor, and had to crane her head a long way up to meet his twinkling eyes. "If you're so fond of getting scratched, make me!"

She had no idea he could move so fast, she thought later, her mouth still burning from the ferocity of his kiss. Her ribs were sore from the strength of his hold as he had pressed her straining body to his, and she was sure she would be black and blue by morning.

"Well . . . well," Cheryl crowed after closing the door behind the departing men. "I thought you said Jace doesn't want you. From what I saw, if we'd left you two huddled over there much longer, you might have offended our sensibilities!"

"Sensibilities be damned," Laura stormed, walking past Cheryl with as much dignity as she could muster. "I'm going to bed."

Slamming her bedroom door to shut out the sound of Cheryl's giggles, Laura quickly undressed. Searching through her bottom drawer, she pulled out an old, well-worn granny nightgown, pulling it over her head with a savage jerk. Examining herself in the mirror, she thought with satisfaction of Jace's expression if he could see her in it. Then she frowned at her reflection. If she knew him, it wouldn't be any use anyway. He would have it off before she knew what hit her.

At the direction her thoughts were taking, she almost ran to the bed, switching off the light on the nightstand with shaking hands. Snuggling beneath the covers, she was sure she wouldn't be able to sleep . . . and abruptly floated off into darkness.

5

The next two days dragged past with unbearable slowness. Jace had had to make an unexpected trip into Sacramento, and she missed him unbearably. She was shocked at her growing dependence, even her sleep disturbed by his image. Last night had been the worst, and had left her bed looking like a war had been fought beneath the covers.

As she showered Saturday morning, she tried to decide what to do with her day. She couldn't face staying alone in the apartment. The walls were becoming palpable enemies to her peace of mind, and she couldn't face the isolation another moment.

Dressing in green-and-blue wool slacks with a matching green sweater, she pulled her hair back, securing it with a leather thong. An intense longing for Jace coursed through her, and she hurried to the phone on the off chance that he had returned from his business trip early. While it rang, she prayed he would answer, but after the sixth ring knew her hopes were futile.

Pacing, Laura realized Jace had achieved his aim where she was concerned, even if he didn't know it yet. He had forced his way into her bloodstream until she needed him . . . wanted him . . . with an intensity that was in itself frightening. But still she struggled with her emotions, vowing not to be like her mother, loving a man to the point of subordinating herself until she had no will of her own.

"Darling, I'm so glad you rang," Irene greeted her at the door. "I was just thinking of calling you. It seems ages since we've spent any time together."

Following Irene up the stairs, Laura frowned. Her mother seemed tense, and she didn't like the pinched look about her mouth. There was a tray on the patio table, and the aroma of freshly brewed coffee emanating from the silver carafe mingled pleasantly with the scent of pine and eucalyptus. She seated herself on a deck chair, studying Irene's nervous movements while listening to her irrelevant and disjointed conversation.

Accepting the coffee her mother handed her, she smiled before lowering her eyes to the rose pattern on the bone-white china.

"Mother, something's wrong," she murmured, taking Irene by surprise. "I don't think I've ever seen you this upset. Is it Father?"

As if in unconcern, Laura started to raise the steaming liquid to her lips, but was halted by a muffled sob. Raising horrified eyes in her mother's direction, she nearly dropped the delicate cup she was holding. Irene had turned her back, to clutch with clawlike fingers at the redwood railing, and her body shook with grief.

Jumping to her feet, Laura reached out, encircling Irene with comforting arms. "My God, Mother, what is it? What's wrong?"

Irene seemed unable to speak, and Laura led her over to a chair.

Eventually Irene began to unburden herself, and as the words tumbled forth from her trembling lips, Laura listened in stunned silence. Another woman? Father . . . ? It just wasn't possible, it couldn't be . . . and she quickly assured her mother that there must be some mistake.

"Do you think I want to believe it?" she cried angrily.

"Mother, I think you're making more of this than you should," Laura asserted. "Father's insanely jealous of anyone who looks cross-eyed at you, and that's not the attitude of a man who wants another woman!"

"Then he's trying to have his cake and eat it too, because I've spoken to her."

Laura stiffened, as much at her mother's tone of voice as at the meaning of her words. So much bitterness . . . a wealth of pain evident in one small sentence, a sentence that, if true, held the power to ruin the life of Irene Spencer!

"Y-you've spoken with this woman? How?"

"Yesterday evening I was home alone when a woman called for Darryl. She seemed upset that I'd answered the phone, said she wanted to speak to your father about seeing him that evening, and then refused to leave a name or number."

"Does Father know?"

"No, I didn't have the nerve to confront him," she replied with shamefaced candor.

"That doesn't prove anything," Laura protested. "Maybe she called to discuss business."

"For all that's holy, Laura," Irene stammered, her lips tightening until they were a thin line in her pale face, "I love your father. Don't you think I'd be the first to give him the benefit of the doubt? For months now I've had the feeling he's been hiding something from me, and now I'm sure of it. The only business those two had to discuss was monkey business, and I won't stand for it. I've put up with a lot over the years, trying to hold a man who has a fatal attraction for women. I've had to be more beautiful, better dressed, and wittier in conversation than anyone else, until I've felt like screaming. Our home had to be kept like a showplace, until I've been afraid to be comfortable. When your father wanted me to accompany him on one of his interminable business trips, I never refused, not wanting to displease him in any way. Because of this, you spent a deprived childhood, lacking both father and mother. Don't you think I've been aware of our selfishness where you were concerned? Well, I have, and believe me, I've agonized over it. You weren't the only one to suffer because of your father's possessiveness. I've suffered too!"

In an excess of pity, Laura observed her mother's face, for the first time noticing tiny wrinkles fanning out beside eyes and mouth, which no amount of cosmetics could hide for long.

Considering her words carefully before she spoke, Laura said, "I never stopped to see things from your point of view. If I had, if only you'd talked to me when I was younger, I would have been more tolerant of the situation, Mother. I'm glad you've suffered, although that sounds cruel, but don't you see," she pleaded, her eyes filling with tears, "it means you love me . . . something I was never sure about."

"To explain would have been to criticize your father, and I've never been capable of that until now. But I've always loved you . . . always," Irene whispered, smoothing Laura's hair with a shaking hand. "You've been my strength, because I always knew that if I was unable to hold your father, you would be there, a part of the love we shared. Oh, darling . . . I'm so glad you came today. I feel as if, somehow, everything's going to be all right now!"

"I know it will, Mother." Laura smiled. "Father couldn't live without you, any more than you could without him. If there is another woman, it won't last long. If you could forgive, I know he'd never leave you."

"Oh, I could forgive, if not forget," Irene murmured wryly, smiling into Laura's eyes as she rose to her feet. "Where he's concerned, I have very little pride."

Laura encouraged her mother to sample a couple of Emma's delicious finger sandwiches, and they talked desultorily, both their minds on other things. Her mother's words about having very little pride kept echoing within the farthest reaches of Laura's mind. Before today she would have looked upon a loss of one's pride as a sign of weakness, but her mother's disclosures had changed all that.

In her own way Irene Spencer was an extremely strong-willed woman, fighting for her man in the only manner she could. She had been strong enough to deny herself the comforts of a normal home life, as well as the company of her only child. If that didn't show a certain kind of strength, what did? Laura wasn't condoning the choice her mother had made, but at least now she was woman enough to understand it. Along with everything else, she could thank Jace for that!

A familiar deep voice interrupted her musings. "I hope you don't mind Emma letting me in, Irene, but I'm in rather a hurry."

Eyes alight with pleasure, Laura jumped to her feet. "Jace, what are you doing here? I thought you were in Sacramento."

She noticed Jace give a start of surprise, and as her eyes met his, she had the uneasy impression he was disconcerted for a brief moment.

With quick strides he reached her, placing a casual arm across her shoulders and dropping a swift kiss on her cheek.

"I had to cancel my last appointment," he explained, his eyes devouring her and bringing a pleased flush to her cheeks. "Miss me?"

"I had no idea that the two of you were . . . were friendly," Irene stammered, watching in fascination the wicked grin Jace gave Laura.

"I'd like to be a lot more than friendly, but so far Laura's still holding out on me, Irene."

"Jace!" Laura wanted to sink through the floor with embarrassment, but to her chagrin, her mother only laughed.

"Even though I'm her mother and shouldn't say this, I can't help hoping you succeed, Jace."

"If the two of you are through discussing me as if I weren't here, maybe Jace can finish telling us why he's come," she snapped, stiffening within the warmth of Jace's embrace.

Laura was sorry for her outburst as she saw her mother's face once again crease in lines of worry and despair.

"Is everything all right, Jace?"

"Sure, Irene," he replied, his eyes softening when encountering the older woman's distress. "Darryl asked me to bring these papers by. They're the plans for the new castings, and he's arranged for Emmerson to pick them up here."

"Why didn't Darryl bring them himself?"

"He's working late and wasn't able to get away," he replied evenly. "He wanted me to let you know that he won't be home until rather late tomorrow night. He said for you not to worry, he intends to sleep at his club."

Laura was never prouder of her mother than she was at that moment. With regal grace, Irene smiled politely at Jace, her glance devoid of inner turmoil.

"It was kind of you to save Darryl the trip," she said, extending her hand. "Thank you, Jace. Now, if you'll just excuse me, I'll go and put these in the safe. Laura will see you out."

Her mother was barely out of sight before Jace turned, his arms reaching around her waist with convulsive pressure. "God, I've missed you!"

Laura returned his caress, her mother's problems momentarily forgotten at the searing pressure of Jace's mouth. She was melting against him, her hands clutching the rippling muscles of his back. She felt rather than heard his groan filling her mouth, and shivered. Returning sanity came when she felt his hands lower to grip her hips, and she couldn't prevent herself from pulling away from the pressure of his demanding arms.

"Jace, don't. I—"

"Dammit, Laura," he exploded, releasing her so suddenly she rocked on her heels and had to grip the edge of a deck chair for balance. "I can't take any more of this!"

His body seemed to shudder violently, and she stared at his broad back with a desperation she couldn't hide. She couldn't blame him for being angry, she thought in disgust. She was no better than the little tease he thought her, responding to him hotly one minute and pulling away the next!

With a smothered oath he turned on his heel, leaving her to stare stupidly after his departing figure. You fool, Laura! Instead of showing him how glad you are to see him, you go and reject him again. How many times will you get away with it before he walks away for good? At the thought, she began running, nearly breaking her neck on the landing. She arrived outside in time to see him lowering himself into his car.

"Jace, please wait," she cried.

At the sound of her voice he straightened and came toward her, his face coldly accusing as he approached the spot where she waited at the bottom of the stairs.

"Well? I'm in a hurry, Laura."

He wasn't going to make it easy for her, that was obvious, she thought, trying to control her breathing as well as an irrational sense of injustice.

"I w-wanted to apologize for what I did in there," she stammered, looking into his harsh countenance pleadingly. "I was upset about something Mother told me, and I just didn't think. I know that's no excuse, but—"

"You're right, it isn't," he growled, clenching his hands. "I've done everything I can to show you what you mean to me, but I'm sick of fighting a losing battle. I can't force your belief."

Her heart was laid bare in her eyes, but he avoided her gaze. Her voice shaking, she whispered, "I believe you."

His features softened miraculously, and she caught her

91

breath as his eyes finally met hers. For wordless seconds they stared at one another, and she felt she would never have enough of just looking at him.

He was wearing a white dress shirt tucked snugly into the waistband of tightly fitting black slacks, sleeves rolled up in response to the warmth of the early spring weather. She reached out, and as her hand made contact with the bareness of his arm, she felt his muscle contract. Her own skin tingled where it brushed against his, and she glanced at him wonderingly, still not able to believe how the most casual touch could make her feel this way.

He bent his head and stared at the whiteness of her hand against his tanned flesh, his mouth curving sensuously.

"Do you want me, Laura?"

The directness of his question left her breathless, as did the expression in his eyes as he waited for her reply. She shook with the force of her emotions, and when she realized that Jace himself was far from unaffected, hope burgeoned within her.

The knowledge served to release her normal reserve. All of a sudden, pride meant less than nothing. If she had to choose between pride and keeping Jace in her life, then there really wasn't a decision to make. A smile curved the softness of her mouth as her lips parted to answer him.

6

~~**e&&&&&&&&&&&&**~~

Darling, aren't you finished yet?" a sulky voice called out across the driveway. "I'm starving!"

The words hovering on Laura's lips were never spoken, as she turned startled eyes toward the stunning woman extricating herself from the passenger side of Jace's car.

"Just a moment longer, Marianna," he answered shortly, giving the svelte figure approaching him a glaring frown.

Undaunted, Marianna slanted him a teasing look from provocative almond-shaped dark eyes. With a single sinuous movement she inserted herself next to him, wrapping her hands possessively around his arm.

Jace had no choice but to introduce the two women. "Laura, this is Marianna Hartley," he snapped impatiently. "Marianna, Laura Spencer, the daughter of my associate, Darryl Spencer."

Laura stared at Jace in disbelieving silence, trying to gauge his reactions from his expression. How could he stand there looking so innocent, when the evidence of his guilt was right beside him? she wondered bitterly. Remembering how she'd accepted his words after dinner the other night, believing him when he had assured her there hadn't been any other women in his life since he'd met her, she felt sick. If Marianna wasn't a woman, then her eyes were deceiving her!

"I'm very happy to meet you, Laura," Marianna simpered, extending a languid hand in Laura's direction.

Ignoring the gesture, Laura summoned her shattered pride and turned to Jace with a disdainful sneer curving her lips.

"When we talked earlier, you should have told me *why* you were in such a hurry."

While they glared at each other like antagonists, Marianna, impatient at being ignored, pouted deliciously curved lips. An expression of disgust crossed Laura's features as she registered the other woman's obviousness. She felt a momentary satisfaction when Jace's jaw tightened after he correctly interpreted her expression.

"I hate to hurry you, darling, but don't you think we'd better be going?"

"Since when do you make my decisions for me, Marianna?" he responded softly, his eyes narrowing with a silent warning.

"I'm sorry," she apologized, turning to Laura with an artful shrug of her rounded shoulders. She deliberately drew attention to the plunging neckline of her gown, which more than amply enhanced the full curves beneath, and Laura felt an insane desire to slap the smug smile from her beautifully made-up face, especially when Marianna continued, "I'm sure Laura understands how it is when a woman's in love, don't you, Laura?"

With a barely perceptible nod of her head, Laura struggled against the pain exploding inside of her. The woman was pure feline, and she wouldn't give her the satisfaction of guessing how deeply her barbs had gouged.

"Marianna, if you . . ." Jace scowled, turning his head from his intent perusal of Laura's strained features.

Without a qualm, Marianna stopped his angry words, lifting his hand to her cheek, a satisfied expression on her face. "Don't be angry with me, darling," she murmured, her voice seductively soft. "Is it my fault you're such a sexy devil? It's selfish of me to begrudge Laura any of your time, especially since I'll have the rest of the night with you, but I'm sure she'll forgive my rudeness."

Her face a polite mask, Laura said, "I won't take up any more of your time, Jace. What I had to say wasn't important."

"Dammit, Laura," he muttered, twisting away from Marianna's clinging hands and moving toward her, "you don't understand. I—"

"I understand perfectly," she retorted, staring at him with mingled dislike and pain. "Thank you for stopping by. Now, if you'll both excuse me . . ."

With as graceful an exit as possible under the circumstances, Laura reentered the house. She felt an eerie calmness settle over her, as if all feeling were suspended, and it suited her just fine.

At least she now knew the reason why he'd been too busy to see her this weekend. He wanted his women willing and eager, she thought, and his girlfriend was that, all right!

As Laura thought of Marianna's warmly inviting body

enclosed in Jace's arms, she felt vicious tendrils of pain curling up inside her.

By eleven o'clock that night Laura was ready to climb the walls. A leisurely soak in the tub hadn't done much to help her relax, but at least it had partially succeeded in filling hours which seemed to move with monotonous slowness.

She had dined with her mother, but refused Irene's offer to spend the night. The emotional apathy she had enjoyed so briefly was wearing off, and she didn't trust herself not to break down and make a fool of herself if she stayed any longer. So far, she had been able to control her emotions; at least she could be thankful for small favors.

But as the hours passed and she thought more and more about Jace's perfidy, numbness was replaced by anger. Jace had a right to as many women as he wanted, but what made her furious was his failure to disclose anything about Marianna's existence. Even when he'd had the opportunity, he'd neglected to say anything, she remembered. Now she knew the agonizing pain her mother was suffering, and she hated herself for feeling anything . . . anything at all!

The more she thought about it, the more obvious it became that Jace was attempting to have her and Marianna both by keeping them apart. It hadn't been part of his plan for her to see them together, but thank God she had! As the thought crossed her mind, tears welled up involuntarily in her eyes, but she fought them back. Maybe the old saying about ignorance being bliss was true, she thought sadly.

The pealing of the doorbell caused her to jump in fright. Her heart was pounding furiously as she walked across the room, and she stood in the entry with indecision written across her features.

This time the reverberation of the bell seemed to go on forever, as if it were being leaned against. She couldn't stand here pretending to be out, but if it was Jace, she didn't have to let him in!

"Who is it?"

"Let me in, Laura," his husky voice demanded. "I want to talk to you."

She greeted the sound of his peremptory demand with a bitter twist of her lips; her body sagged limply against the wall. "I'm sorry, but I'm too tired to listen to you. We'll have to talk some other time." What a liar I am, she thought. She had no intention of ever speaking to him again!

The knob rattled furiously, and Jace's voice was even louder than before. "Laura, I'm warning you," he hissed, and she jumped at the sound of an open palm slamming against wood.

"Is Marianna with you?" Her mouth was curved in a saccharine smile, which widened when she heard him uttering an apparently endless string of curses.

Laura frowned as she suddenly heard other sounds from the corridor.

"Here, you, get away from there!"

With her ear pressed close, she heard Jace attempting to explain his presence.

"Yeah, I'll bet," another voice mocked. "Come on, mister, you can save your explanations for the cops."

A nervous giggle escaped her. Although she was sorely

tempted, she couldn't subject Jace to the indignity of trying to explain himself to the authorities, and slowly she opened the door.

"It's all right." She smiled at the night watchman. "This man's a friend of my father's."

Glancing at Jace for the first time, she nearly changed her mind and told the uniformed guard to take him away. If he could get his hands on her, he would strangle her, she was sure of it!

The guard looked doubtfully at Jace. "Are you sure, miss? He sounded pretty threatening to me."

With a feeling of horror, Laura noticed the gun in the man's hand, which was pointed in the direction of Jace's chest. "Don't point that thing at him," she yelped. "It might go off!"

Insulted by the reprimand, the guard slowly returned his gun to its holster. "Only doing my job," he retorted, dividing his disgusted glance equally between the two of them. "If he's such a friend, why wouldn't you let him in?"

"A lovers' tiff, Officer," Jace remarked smoothly, moving to drape his arm casually across Laura's tense shoulders. "You know how women are!"

"Don't I just." The man grinned, flattered by Jace's mode of address. "My old woman's the same, she is," he confided with a wink in Jace's direction which made Laura want to hit him. "You're gettin' off light, fella. Mine usually throws something at me. Caught me a real cropper the other evening, just because I had me a little bit of a game with the boys."

"If you two are quite through comparing your life stories, I'd like to go to bed!"

"Now, that's a suggestion any man would be eager to

comply with," Jace murmured, caressing her neck with his hand. Flinching from his touch, she raised her head to glare at him, a retort quivering on her lips. Before she could say a word, he forestalled her by lowering his mouth to hers in a brief kiss.

"Humph," the guard coughed. "I'll be on my way, then. Sorry for the mistake."

"That's all right, Officer," Jace replied, almost pushing Laura through the doorway. "Good night!"

Storming into the living room, Laura rounded on him, her eyes twin storm signals in her flushed face. "You had no right! Now he thinks . . . he thinks we're . . ."

"Sleeping together?" Jace questioned softly, removing his coat with apparent unconcern and draping it careless-ly over the end of the couch. "He'd be right."

At his calm assertion, Laura's breath caught in her throat, and she backed nervously away from his slowly approaching figure.

"You have a lot of nerve," she spluttered, clutching at the pulse jumping in her throat. "Isn't one woman a night enough for you?"

"If you happen to be that woman." The eyes holding hers blazed with unmistakable intent as he closed the distance between them.

"Go back to Marianna," she cried, goaded beyond endurance by the clean, musky scent of his body pressing hers against the wall. "She's quite sickeningly eager to satisfy your desires."

"You're the only one who'll satisfy me, Laura," he replied quietly, tangling his hands in her disordered hair and forcing her to face him.

Gripping his wrists, she attempted to loosen his hold on her hair, conceding defeat when she could no longer stand the painful tugging at her temples. She felt at a disadvantage, aware as she was of her own nakedness beneath the gray silk caftan she wore. That he suspected her vulnerability was obvious from the narrowing of his eyes, which raked over her with a heat she could almost feel penetrating the softly clinging folds.

"I couldn't care less about whether or not you're satisfied." Laura attempted to push against his chest. "Marianna might be pleased to accept your loathsome touch, but I'm not. Just get out of here!"

With a muffled curse he lowered his hands, gripping her arms and encircling her body completely when she fell against him.

At the sudden contact, Laura's thinly held control snapped. Her nails raked his back through the fine cambric of his shirt, her slippered feet having little or no effect upon his legs as she attempted to kick him with vicious intent.

"Let me go," she sobbed bitterly. "You're hurting me!"

"Then quit behaving like a little shrew."

"Since I'm forced to endure your company, do you think I might sit down?"

Smiling at the sarcasm, he brushed her hair back from her flushed cheeks. "Certainly," he murmured, and she gave a little gasp as he lifted her in his arms, swift strides quickly eliminating the distance to the divan in the corner.

"Let me up," she stormed, trying to struggle off his lap. When she tried pounding at him, he grasped her wrists in one large hand, using his other to encircle her waist, tugging until she was half-sitting, half-lying across his thighs.

"Will you behave yourself?" he laughed, his mouth disturbingly close. "Last time you squirmed like that, I told you I wouldn't be responsible for my actions."

"You're an animal," she snapped, forcing her body into stillness.

"No, only a man who wants you badly." He grinned with a wry quirk of his eyebrows.

Flushing, she suddenly became all too aware of his desire for her and raised startled eyes to his. Shared awareness rippled between them, as heat flooded every pore of her body.

"Didn't you believe me when I said I wanted you?" he questioned softly.

Breaking free of his glance, she stared instead at his chest, although the brief glimpse she had of black hair where his collar parted did nothing to still her churning emotions.

"You only know one word—'want,'" she said, turning her head away and gazing mutinously into the distance.

"Damn you, do you think it's been easy for me, going so slow with you . . . trying to understand your reluctance? You needed time, and I promised myself you should have it. The challenge, if you want to call it that, was in stopping myself from barging in here and following my instincts. Instead, I've been patient, and look where it got me!"

This last was spoken with such a wealth of bitter irony, she looked at him in amazement. The anger of just moments before seemed to have drained out of him, and he rested his head against the back of the couch, closing his eyes. His lips were pressed tightly together as if with pain at his thoughts, and before she could think about it, her hand pressed against him fleetingly.

Her shoulders were seized in a relentless grip, and he muttered harshly, "Don't play with me, Laura. I've taken about as much as I can stand."

Hurt beyond measure at his rejection of her innocent attempt at comfort, she sat up stiffly, starting to get to her feet.

With a groan he pulled her against him, his mouth feathering brief, shattering kisses over her face and neck.

"Jace, you can't . . . Please," she pleaded, fighting the urges of her own body.

"Please," he moaned against her throat. "That's all I want, to please you until you're as sick with love for me as I am for you."

Leaning back once again, he withdrew his hands. His fingers rested with assumed casualness on the overstuffed arm of the divan, and his eyes roamed the delicacy of her features intently.

"I first fell for a furiously spitting kitten who had the audacity to insult me over the phone." He smiled, his voice gentle. "I manipulated our meeting, and when I saw you standing beside your mother with your eyes shooting green fire, I was lost. I'll be honest with you, honey. I fought against my feelings like hell, assuring myself that once I'd bedded you I could put you behind me as easily as all the other women I've known."

"So I was right," she muttered, turning her head aside so he couldn't see her face. "You were plotting an affair all along!"

Grasping her chin, he turned her face toward his. "If I hadn't cared more about your feelings than my own, we'd be lovers by now, Laura."

Laura bit her lip, her eyes troubled. His words were true. Even the night of her birthday, he could have had her—if he had persisted. She wouldn't have had the strength to resist, she admitted. Still, she thought, where in the world did Marianna figure in all of this?

She voiced the question, and gasped when his fingers tightened painfully upon her chin.

"At the time I met you, Marianna was my mistress, and had been for some time."

At his words her eyes closed in an effort to force back her tears, and her lips trembled uncontrollably. She had guessed the truth, but hearing him confirm her suspicions was another matter entirely. She couldn't stomach the idea of Marianna in his arms, or the thought that he had come from his mistress to her.

"There's no more to be said, then. I don't want any kind of relationship with you, Jace . . . not anymore. I don't like the idea of being just another one of your women. One mistress should be enough for any man!"

"Dammit, Laura," he cursed, his face grim. "I broke it off with Marianna shortly after we met. I'm a man with the usual urges, not some sex-crazed maniac."

"Tell me another one," she responded bitterly. "I'm not blind, or was the woman drooling all over you today a figment of my imagination?"

Taking him by surprise, she jumped to her feet. With her hands clenched tightly, she had to forcibly restrain herself from aiming one of them at his formidable jaw.

"Come back here," he gritted from between clenched teeth, "and quit acting like a child."

He caught up with her in the dining room, grabbing her arm and swinging her around to face him. Other than that one brief contact he didn't attempt to touch her. Instead, he jammed his fists into his black slacks with a violent movement.

"I have my pride, Laura, so I'll say this just once. I am not sleeping with Marianna, and I'm not in the habit of lying!"

Moistening her parched lips with the tip of her tongue, she tried to read the closed expression on his face. His words had been spoken so dispassionately, as if he were quickly reaching the point of not caring whether she believed him or not.

"It . . . it was obvious the two of you planned on being together tonight," she protested, lowering her head and studying the tips of the gray slippers peeping beneath her hem.

"I'm here. . . . Doesn't that prove anything to you?"

"Oh, God . . . I don't know what to believe," she cried, turning her back and moving a few steps away. She couldn't concentrate with him so close! She didn't hear his soft-footed approach, and jumped when she felt his hands against her taut shoulders.

"Don't, Jace. Don't touch me . . . I can't stand it!"

"So we're back to square one." His voice sounded tired and defeated.

A piercing pain sliced through her, and with an anguished cry she raised her hands to her face, pressing against her closed eyelids in an attempt to ease the pressure building there.

"What do you expect from me?" she moaned, shaking her head in a negative gesture. "You forced your way into my life. I couldn't cope with the things you were making me feel, but when you weren't around anymore, I found myself unable to accept your absence, either. I know I asked you to go, and I thought it was the right thing at the time. Then, when I'd realized my mistake, it was too late to do anything about it. I've been so miserable, and now

I'm not even able to trust my own decisions any longer. I want to believe you—you don't know how much. It's your fault I can't. You should have told me about Marianna when we were at my parents' house, instead of waiting until I saw you together. If I hadn't followed you, I'd be as much in the dark as ever!"

"What was I supposed to say, Laura? My ex-mistress is waiting for me in the car, but I'll explain later?"

"That's another thing," she remarked with stubborn persistence. "You have to admit that her presence makes your story a little difficult to believe!"

"Dammit, Laura. She hasn't accepted our separation at all gracefully. She's even shown up at my place a couple of times, but I don't relish being hunted any more than the next man, and I left her in no doubt of my feelings. She knew the score from the beginning," he growled, as Laura protested his harsh treatment of the other woman with an involuntary cry, "so don't bother feeling sorry for her. Our relationship was on a business footing from the start, and believe me, I paid well for pleasures received. She showed up at the foundry yesterday, begging me for help. She has a penchant for roulette, and managed to get herself in quite a mess. In view of our past association, I've agreed to bail her out one more time. She handed the notes over to me at the restaurant this evening, I put her in a cab, and that's the end of it as far as I'm concerned."

His explanation was too fantastic not to be true, she thought. She wanted so much to believe that his relationship with the other woman was over, but the seeds of distrust sown in her marriage to Phillip made it agonizingly difficult. The reasons she had judged Jace so harshly were logical ones, but that didn't justify her attitude, she thought, as she remembered lecturing her mother about understanding and forgiveness. Shame coursed through her, and she wrapped her arms together across her chest. The real reason for her close-minded attitude washed over her, and she found it difficult to face up to her own stupidity.

"I . . . I wanted to believe her lies," she whispered, averting her face. "I've been afraid of committing myself. I . . . I'm sorry. I don't know what else to say. . . ."

By the time the last word passed her taut lips, she could no longer meet his eyes. She stiffened as his hands grasped her, sliding warmly to engulf her crossed arms within his.

"Laura, don't . . ." he groaned, pulling her shaking body against his hard warmth. "After all that garbage Marianna gave you, I can't blame you for believing what you did. What hurt me was your unwillingness to allow me to explain. I need your trust desperately, darling. Marianna said what she did deliberately to get even with me for dropping her. I almost told her to go fly her own kite," he said, his disgust apparent in his voice, "but she got hysterical. It took me a while to calm her down. That's why I was so long getting here."

The image his words created in her mind released the coil of tension knotting her stomach, and she began to laugh. She could just see Jace, his dignity in shreds as he tried to calm a hysterical female in a crowded restaurant.

Jace stiffened at the sound of her laughter. When she saw his indignant expression, she laughed all the harder.

"I'm s-sorry," she gulped, choking on the words. "Y-you must have looked so funny, with Marianna w-weeping all over you, and . . . and everybody s-staring."

Jace drew her toward him and cradled her in his arms. "You think it's funny, do you?" His eyes lingered on her lips, while one lean finger gently traced their outline. "It's not polite to laugh at someone else's misfortune, kitten. I think you deserve some punishment, and I'm just the man to do it!"

She lowered her fascinated gaze from the devilment leaping in his eyes, her laughter replaced by a burgeoning excitement. She swallowed convulsively as his head descended, all rational thought ceasing as his hard mouth parted the soft willingness of hers.

At the touch of their mingled flesh, what had begun as a teasing exploration swiftly turned into something more . . . much more. Jace's tongue thrust aggressively within the warm cavern of her mouth, and when she moaned her response, his movements became almost frenzied.

Her hands clutched at his hair, causing pleasure and pain to ripple through him as they rocked together. His legs were parted for balance, while his kneading fingers clutched the rounded smoothness below her waist, pressing her against him.

His breath rasped as he pulled away to stare into her expressive face, arousal deepening upon observing the hectic flush of her answering desire. This was the way he'd dreamed of seeing her—eyes clouded with emotion, hair rippling over her body like fire, mouth parted softly, eager for the glide of his tongue.

Laura's eyes closed, unable to withstand his knowing scrutiny, and an unintelligible murmur of protest escaped her.

"No! Don't turn away . . . I want to look at you," he groaned, his hands moving urgently upon the fastening of her caftan. "I want to see every inch of you

107

. . . glistening cream mingling with moist shadows . . . not just imagine them. You're the reality of all my fantasies, Laura . . . and I love you . . . I love you . . ." He was tense, releasing his breath on a sigh when she offered no resistance. He began lowering the gown from her shoulders. "Give me my dream, honey," he breathed, "and I'll share it with you."

Laura's eyes remained closed as the flowing silk slithered down her body and dropped to a pool at her feet in glistening disarray. All she was conscious of was an intense desire to please him.

That he would be gaining his pleasure at her expense, she never for a second believed. By her reaction to his skilled caresses, she was certain that in giving she would receive much more than just a share of the delight his hoarse words promised.

"Dear God!"

Just a strangled exclamation, but it was enough to awaken her from the abstraction of her thoughts. It's too soon! Her mind uttered the protest even as she was lifted high in his arms. His mouth burned feverishly against her temple as he carried her in the direction of her darkened bedroom. Mouth dry, she deliberately looked anywhere but at the shadowy form of Jace's rippling torso as he stood her on her feet and removed his own clothing.

"What is it . . . what's wrong, Laura?"

Trapped in her own hesitant doubts, she hadn't felt Jace's weight depress the bed as he lowered her and then lay beside her. She didn't know how to answer his question, or even if she knew the answers. She wanted to hide in the darkness forever, she thought. How could she tell him that she didn't know what she wanted? Would he understand her need for a little more time before making this last, irrevocable step forward in their relationship?

She shook her head in mute despair, then felt the bed tilt as Jace rose to his feet, a resigned sigh accompanying his movements.

"Put this on!"

Obligingly, without a word of protest, Laura raised her arms as Jace lowered her discarded gown over her head. Emerging from the folds, she was startled at the sight of his bare flesh, following the line of chest hair downward with her eyes until it disappeared within the waistband of his shorts. She once again raised her gaze to his, staring at him silently as he ordered, "Move over!"

With a wry twist to his mobile mouth, he sat down beside her. She couldn't tear her gaze from his face, and at her look of silent anguish he gathered her against him.

"It's all right, babe . . . don't look at me like that," he muttered, tilting her head back until he could see her face. "I shouldn't have rushed you. We've just begun to understand our feelings for each other, so let's not force a physical union until we're *both* ready to enjoy it, hmmm?"

"You should hate me," she admitted, her hand caressing his face.

"You little fool . . ." He smiled, nipping playfully at her fingers with his teeth. "I'll regret this in the morning, but when we make love, you're going to be completely ready for me!"

"I love you, Jace."

His face softened as she at long last admitted her feelings for him. Laura expelled her breath in a sigh, as if by committing herself a great weight was lifted from her.

"Are you going to move over, or do I have to shove you?"

"Wh-what?"

"I don't know about you"—he grinned, scooping her into his arms and depositing her on the opposite side of the bed—"but I'm tired. I need my rest, woman!"

The latter was spoken with a little-boy plaintiveness, and Laura chuckled as he lowered his body beside her.

"You're forever laughing at me," he growled, lifting her to lie against the warmth of his shoulder. "Someday I'm going to make you pay for that!"

Eventually, with Jace's low-murmured words rumbling in her ear, Laura relaxed fully. She snuggled her warm, pliant body against him, her lids growing heavier as she tried to continue listening. The effort became more and more difficult, until with a soft sigh of contentment she slept in his arms. It was a long, long time before Jace was finally able to join her.

7

Laura was fighting a losing battle to remain unconscious, floating half-asleep in the insidious languor which held her enthralled. Squirming pleasurably back against the enjoyable warmth surrounding her, she lost the battle entirely when a deep chuckle greeted her movements.

"Mmmm, don't stop, sweetheart," Jace whispered, his mouth against the back of her neck. "It feels good!"

"That's the trouble," she quipped, but her laughter was abruptly stifled when the covers were thrown back and his hand connected with her backside.

"Why did you do that, you beast?"

"Because the beast would have remained asleep if you hadn't deliberately prodded him awake," he chuckled, lowering his head and using his mouth to trace the gentle path his fingers were traveling.

"Does that make it better, little cat?"

"Jace, please," she moaned, fighting against his restricting hold.

"Please?" His voice posed the question with silky

insistence, his mouth once again upon the sensitive cord of her neck.

"Yes, please . . . damn you," she stormed, his teasing driving her beyond the limits of her endurance to withstand him. "Let me get up," she demanded.

"If you move, the beast might get you," he warned, and she longed to punch him.

"I can take care of the beast!"

"I know you can." He laughed, making her jump when his hand once again slapped her still-smarting rear, her surprise increasing when she felt him leave the bed. "The beast would like nothing better, but we don't have time."

Reaching for the sheet, she pulled it against her chest as she sat up, her eyes turning to him with puzzled inquiry.

"Time for what?"

"I thought we'd take a run to Monterey today."

"Well, thanks for asking," she retorted, her mouth mutinous.

"You're welcome," he mocked, his smile increasing as he studied her expression. "Since you're such a lazy kitten, I'll use the bathroom first."

The light of battle was in her eyes as she measured the distance to the bathroom door before making a run for it. To her chagrin, her feet tangled in the trailing folds of the blankets, and she would have fallen ignominiously at his feet if he hadn't caught her.

Laughing helplessly, she relaxed within the tight security of his arms, until he silenced her chuckles quite effectively with a hard kiss. Just as her knees turned to water, he held her away from him, a triumphant gleam dancing in the depths of his silver eyes.

He was playing with her, arousing her and then holding her off by turns. He was the most infuriating, frustrating . . . She resented his composure, especially since she herself was a shaking mass of longing. She lowered her eyes from his knowing glance . . . and caught her breath. A smug smile erased the petulance of her expression.

"I'm hungry."

"I know!"

A grin tugged the corner of his mouth upward, and she found the slanting smile devastatingly attractive. Tenderly she traced the outline of his mouth, yelping when his strong white teeth clamped down on the offending member in a teasing bite.

"I meant for food, woman, although if you're offering to be a substitute, I wouldn't mind having you instead," he growled.

Still uncertain of her own abilities in that direction, Laura backed down from the question in his eyes. "I . . . If you let me use the bathroom first, I can cook your breakfast while you shower."

"I've got a better idea. Why don't we shower together —just to save on your water bill, of course."

"I have the money to pay my bills," she responded nervously, backing away from him. "You needn't worry."

"If I promise to behave myself?"

He was like a small boy begging for a treat, and she responded to the teasing question with a smile. "You can promise all you like," she retorted, moving past him into the bathroom and beginning to close the door, "but from what I've seen, you have very little control over the beast in you!"

The sound of his laughter lingered in her mind as she showered, and as the water cooled her heated body she laughed aloud with happiness. She was finding it exhilarating to test his reactions to provocation. She knew she was playing with fire, but for the first time in her life she almost welcomed the idea of being blasted by the fire of passion.

"If you're not out of there in one minute flat, I'm going to come in after you," Jace warned, pounding resoundingly on the door.

Taking a deep breath, Laura willed her expression into one of cool composure, making sure the large bath towel was wrapped securely around her before releasing the catch on the door.

"The bathroom's all yours," she murmured, moving past his still figure with regal precision. "You'll find a package of disposable razors under the basin cabinet."

She was almost out of reach, and feeling inordinately pleased with herself for evening the score between them, when she felt a forceful tug on the back of the towel. It was too late to grasp the tucked ends as the towel was jerked from around her, and once again she felt his hand connecting with her bottom. She wondered furiously if he had a thing about that particular part of her anatomy, blushing furiously when she suddenly remembered his caressing hands applying soothing comfort after his earlier punishment.

With a gasp she whirled around, only to be faced with a firmly closed door.

"You . . . you beast," she yelled, a closed fist pounding on the panel.

"That's right, honey," he chuckled. "Do you want to come in here and tame me?"

At his teasing challenge, Laura's own sense of humor was revived, and she met his muffled laughter with her own.

"No thanks," she retorted, tossing her head disdainfully while walking toward the closet.

"Chicken!"

Carefree laughter was to set the seal upon their day together, a day that was the happiest Laura could ever remember spending.

The drive down the coast was filled with warmth and a shared intimacy she had never known. Jace's conversation was laced with undertones, his eyes constantly reminding her of the moments spent in his arms. She responded timidly at first, and then with growing confidence. This seemed to please him, and she basked in the warmth of his approval.

It was late in the afternoon when they finally approached the small community of Monterey nestling snugly in the arms of the bay. Jace drove to the intersection of Franklin and Camino El Estero on the eastern edge of town.

Apparently Jace was extremely knowledgeable about Monterey. He told Laura of his boyhood days, and summers spent with a favorite uncle on the outskirts of town in a cabin with few modern conveniences. Laura sensed the pain behind his words: pain caused by a father too busy to adapt his energies to those of a small boy.

"How could your mother tolerate never seeing you?" she cried, indignant at the idea of a child being completely ignored in that way. At least her own mother, though rarely there, had insisted on Laura being raised within the

115

security of her own home. Boarding school had come later, not when she was little more than a baby!

Glancing at him out of the corner of her eye, she noticed how grim Jace's expression had become. A muscle jumped in his cheek, as if he were biting down hard with clenched teeth.

"My mother died at my birth," he responded quietly. "The old man couldn't stand the sight of me after that. As an infant I was in the care of a nurse, and as soon as I was old enough, I was sent to school."

"How could he?"

At the sound of her appalled whisper, Jace's head swiveled in her direction, his expression softening when he noticed her agitation.

"I don't blame him, honey. He loved my mother, and blamed himself for her death. If she hadn't become pregnant, she'd be alive today. I was a reminder of his guilt. I'm not saying he was right, only that he couldn't help himself."

"I'm sorry, Jace."

"Sorry . . . what are you talking about?" He placed his arm around her shoulders and pulled her close beside him.

"I'm sorry for thinking you a golden boy, seeing you only as a man like my father, ruthless with ambition. I never imagined that you were even lonelier than I was as a child."

"Be grateful, honey," he whispered, feathering a kiss against her temple. "Your loneliness matched mine, drawing us together whether we wanted to be drawn or not. If you look hard enough, my old uncle used to tell me, you can find good in the worst situations."

"I would have liked your uncle, I think."

"He would have loved you, the old reprobate." He chuckled. "He had an eye for a beautiful woman."

Slapping his wandering hand, she placed a necessary distance between them. "That must be where you get it, then!"

Jace's laughter rang in her ears while she tugged her white cable-knit pullover down over black wool slacks. He hadn't allowed her to put her hair up for their outing, so she'd compromised by twisting it into one long plait down her back. Glaring at him, she tossed the errant plait over her shoulder, turning to study the passing scenery as if fascinated.

Within moments, though, Laura's fascination wasn't feigned. The Path of History was delineated by historical markers, which Laura studied eagerly. Soon she became engrossed in the sight of the old buildings, eagerly soaking up Spanish-Mexican-American history. Amused at her eagerness, Jace answered her questions willingly, and at the completion of the drive she felt a unity with the past, as if she could actually feel what had gone on in this sea-guarded old city of California.

"You hungry?"

Turning bemused eyes in his direction, Laura nodded.

"How about eating at Fisherman's Wharf?"

"I'd love it, but aren't we going in the wrong direction?"

"If you won't flay me alive for such sacrilege, we can always go back . . . only faster."

Laura's eyes sparkled wickedly. "You're a philistine!"

Using a convenient wide shoulder to turn the car in the proper direction, Jace grinned. "No, but my stomach is!"

Seafood smells mingled with the tangy odor of the sea as they walked out of the parking lot and onto the wharf.

The day was cold, and she was glad that Jace had insisted she take her gold fur-lined parka. They had stopped by his house briefly, and he had been amused when she opted to wait in the car while he changed into warmer clothing. Looking at him now, devastating in tan slacks and gold velour shirt open at the throat, his own zip-fronted jacket in chocolate brown hanging open, she felt the wait had been well worth it. He was a handsome devil as he strode freely beside her, and she enjoyed the envious looks of the women they passed. Their eyes were drawn like magnets to the masculine beauty of his tanned face, lingering almost imperceptibly upon the startling white wings which fanned his temples.

"I think we'd better get a snack at that stall to tide us over," he murmured. "Hunger is making you look quite ferocious!"

They were passing the edge of the marina when he spoke, and the retort she was about to utter was never made, as her attention was caught by the area. They were traversing a sculptured walk, and although the water in the ocean ebb was murky and dark, it was threaded with small bright fish moving in schools. Colored shells with spidery little creatures in them were scuttling on the rocks, and she was fascinated by the display of life in a bay which was an ecological wreck, killed by civilization.

Laura mentioned this to Jace, who told her of the studies being made at the Hopkins Marine Station, by Cannery Row, in an attempt to discover the reasons for the demise of the bay.

"We'll stop by Cannery Row if we have the time," he promised.

"Jace, couldn't we have dinner there? There are some

lovely seafood restaurants, and it's one of my favorite places," she pleaded.

"Ahh, a Steinbeck fan, are you?"

"He's one of my favorites," she admitted, stopping beside him while he ordered tiny baskets of shrimp from a sidewalk vendor.

Handing her one small basket, he laughed when her nose wrinkled in appreciation of the teasing aroma wafting upward.

"He's my favorite, too," he surprised her by saying. "He made Monterey famous with his writings. I think the best description ever written about any place was Steinbeck's description of Cannery Row."

"I know," she exclaimed, her smile matching his own as she quoted several lines from Steinbeck's work.

"I knew there was a reason why I love you," he murmured.

Her hand paused in midair as she met the seriousness of his expression. A juicy, succulent shrimp dangled from the edge of a wooden prong, and with a husky laugh he took the utensil from her unresisting fingers. She opened her mouth automatically, and he popped the offering between her lips.

"Lucky shrimp," he sighed, his mouth quirking upward in the slanted smile for which she was beginning to hunger.

Approaching Cannery Row, Laura was conscious of a familiar sense of sadness. Steinbeck wrote about the Row with such an empathy and a sense of rightness that the six-block-long piece of harbor front became world-famous overnight. Now it was all changed. The sardines were gone, in one of those mysteries of sea nature, and the canneries had shuttered doors, boarded against intruders, broken windows, with the corrugated iron peeling away from the bones of the vast warehouses.

Dinner was a leisurely meal, which Laura enjoyed immensely. Jace insisted she try first one offering and then another, and her taste buds overrode common sense. When he ordered a dessert with their coffee, of shaved chocolate and whipped cream, all she could do was glare at him threateningly.

Laura walked out of the restaurant replenished both in body and spirit. Until that moment she hadn't been aware of the swiftly passing time, and was startled by the descending twilight which greeted their exit. A cold wind off the sea caused her to hug her coat tightly around her, but she was soon warmed by the brisk pace Jace set as they hurried to the car.

Jace's car ate up the miles much too quickly. Soon she would be home, and she couldn't bear the thought of being separated from Jace. In startled awareness she glanced at him, eyes wide with the knowledge of how necessary he was to her peace of mind.

To her consternation, Jace intercepted her glance, and although she quickly averted her face, she knew he read the naked longing in her expression. A tense silence filled the warmth of the car, the only sound the gentle hum of the heater. Clenching her hands tightly together, she resisted the urge to blurt out her thoughts, and felt like a fool when Jace shifted his weight on the plush seat beside her, causing her to jump like a startled rabbit.

"Will you sleep with me tonight, Laura?"

Startled, she stared at him in disbelief. Although he had affirmed his love for her, there had never been any mention of permanency in their relationship, and she felt his question unfair.

"I was being straight with you, babe," he replied, glancing at her swiftly before returning his gaze to the traffic ahead. "If I had asked you to my place for a drink, you would have agreed."

"But—"

"No, Laura, don't interrupt," he demanded, his tone firm. "You would have agreed, and eventually I would have tried to get you in bed . . . you know that I want you. I'm not about to be blamed for seducing you later, when you've had time to think. When we make love, it will be with our eyes open . . . with both of us knowing what we want. Why do you think I didn't finish what you so deliciously started this morning? I'll tell you why, honey . . . because it wouldn't have been fair. A woman's at her most vulnerable when she's just been wakened from sleep, her body relaxed and receptive. I want everything from you, maybe more than you're willing to give right now . . . and until I hear you admit you want me as well as love me, our relationship will just have to remain as it is."

"Would that be so terrible?" she questioned, her voice little more than a whisper.

"It would be hell," he rasped, his hands clenching the steering wheel tightly. "I'm not used to a celibate existence, Laura, and you've got me so tied up in knots that at times I feel as if I'm going to go crazy."

"I haven't got a monopoly on you, Jace. There are other women—"

Laura gasped as Jace, with a savage jerk on the wheel, pulled the car to the side of the road. As it rolled to a halt she felt his hands on her shoulders in a violent grip, and her eyes dilated as she stared into the wrathful depths of his.

"Damn you, is that what you want?"

"P-please, I didn't mean—"

"Believe me, your meaning came through loud and clear," he said, and she flinched at the disgust in his voice. "I'll take you home, Laura. I've been a fool, thinking I could ever penetrate that barrier of pride you've erected around yourself. I want to marry you, but I'm damned if I'll have a wife who doesn't care whose bed I sleep in, as long as it isn't hers!"

Shock kept her rigid as they drove the remaining distance. His wife . . . he wanted her to be his wife! She had almost made a dreadful mistake, but surely it wasn't too late to rectify it!

"I'll . . . I'll marry you, Jace." She hated herself for the timidness of her words, especially when he ignored her and took the exit to her apartment in silence.

"D-did you hear what I said?"

"I heard you!"

"Then why don't you say something?"

Pulling up outside, Jace still hadn't answered her question. They reached the door to her apartment in tense disharmony, and she felt herself shaking as she fumbled within her purse for the key. She couldn't look at him, and was unprepared when he took the key from her hand, pushing open the door and motioning her ahead of him. With determined steps he moved toward the phone and lifted the receiver.

"At dinner the other night Frank mentioned that he and Cheryl would be going to Reno for a couple of days. Where are they staying?"

"At Harrah's . . . why?"

"Won't you want Cheryl to be your maid of honor?" Slanting her his rakish grin, he began dialing. Well, what else could she expect from such a barbarian? she thought, her mouth curving in a relieved smile. From the very beginning he'd taken over, sweeping away not only her objections to him but also her will to resist.

Jace motioned her to his side, and then handed her the receiver. Frowning in puzzlement, she nearly squirmed when she heard her mother's voice. With Jace's arm around her, his hand absently caressing the flowing line of her hip, she found it very difficult answering her mother's excited questions. Finally, with Irene's congratulations ringing in her ears, she lowered the phone, wanting to slap the smug look from Jace's face. Before she could act out the urge, he was once again dialing, this time to Reno, Nevada.

"Frank? . . . No, everything's great, or nearly. Listen, could you do me a favor? Laura and I are going to be married and I'd like you to be best man. Will you call around and make the arrangements for us? . . . When? Tomorrow, if you can swing it."

As soon as he replaced the phone and turned to her, she was ready to murder him. "I'd like to know what you think you're doing."

"I'm arranging to marry you as soon as possible."

"Don't I have anything to say about it, or are you going to go through this without me?"

The satisfied expression on his face changed to one of bewildered concern. "I thought you wanted to get married," he murmured, eyes dancing devilishly as he drew her stiffly protesting form closer.

"I do, so wipe that silly look off your face, Jace Matthews. The only thing I'm objecting to is your haste!"

His husky laugh shivered along her nerve ends, and she almost hated herself for giving him so much control over her. She wasn't about to let herself become a doormat for any man—least of all a self-willed, irritating . . .

Her thoughts were lost as soon as his mouth touched hers, his lips teasing her own until nothing seemed to matter very much, except that she didn't want him to stop.

"Just think, honey," he whispered against her mouth. "When I'm your husband, you'll have the right to rant at me during the nights as well as the days. Won't that make you happy?"

"Immensely, as long as you remember who's boss," she retorted.

"I am!"

"In a pig's eye!"

Seizing her in a hug she was sure cracked a couple of ribs, he whirled her around the floor until she pleaded with him to stop.

"What will you give me if I do?"

"Myself," she dimpled, her arms locked around his neck as if she would never let go.

Deliberately lowering her slowly down the muscular length of his body, he held her still for long moments while his eyes burned a silent message into her brain.

"Let's go," he groaned, "before I'm tempted to collect in advance!"

8

Their wedding day dawned crisp and clear, bright sunlight coloring the landscape with surrealistic images which were to remain in Laura's mind during the brief but poignant ceremony which made her Jace's wife. The chapel was decorated with big bunches of flowers, the altar a whitely gleaming backdrop to their fragrant beauty.

By the time all of the formalities were completed and the two couples were once again standing outside the small chapel, it was nearly four o'clock. The wedding had been scheduled for three, which had given Cheryl enough time to drag Laura to a conveniently nearby boutique, where her wedding outfit was purchased.

Smoothing the gleaming folds of the oyster satin gown with its overlay of delicate lace, she was glad Cheryl had convinced her to buy it. As they drove to the restaurant Jace had chosen for their wedding celebration, she smiled as she remembered the warm glow in his eyes when he first saw her wearing it. Her hair was swept back in a demure chignon, except for the small curly tendrils nestling at her temples, and she knew she was looking her best.

Frank had ordered champagne. Jace's eyes met hers during the ensuing toast to their happiness, and at the warm promise glinting within their silver depths, Laura felt the breath catch in her throat. She was almost relieved when Cheryl laughed at the two of them, accusing them of making sheep's eyes at each other.

"Could we go to the dinner show tonight?" Laura asked Jace as they passed a marquee advertising the appearance of a well-known celebrity during their drive back to the casino. "I have all his records, and I'd love to see him in person."

"Trying to put off the evil moment, honey?"

"Of course not," she protested, not meeting his eyes. "I really would like to hear him."

He smiled at her reassuringly before glancing into the rearview mirror. "Frank, how does dinner and a show sound to you?"

"Fine, but are you sure you want the two of us horning in?"

"If I didn't think Laura would enjoy herself more with you two along, I wouldn't have asked," he drawled, pulling into a parking space while slanting Laura a mocking smile.

As Laura entered the main foyer of the casino with Jace's fingers threaded through hers, her eyes were alight with love.

By that evening, Laura found herself staring bemusedly at the stage, lost to the sounds around their table. Jace seemed to be amused by her enthusiasm, his eyes twinkling as she turned to him after the performance.

"You were eating him with your eyes, and I resent it," he drawled, one finger sliding provocatively along her inner arm. "I'm not worried, though," he continued, his eyes capturing hers as they flickered from the effects of his caress. "By tomorrow you'll be looking at me like that."

Gulping, she took a deep breath, determined not to allow him to guess the depth of his power over her churning emotions. "You certainly don't suffer from an inferiority complex, do you!"

"I haven't had any complaints." He chuckled softly when his reply brought fire shooting from her emerald eyes.

He sat back in his chair, a quietly satisfied expression on his face, and she longed to hit him over the head with something.

"You ready to leave, honey?"

At Jace's question, she jumped visibly. "Oh, where are we going now?"

"Where do you think?"

Cheryl and Frank burst into laughter, and she turned to them indignantly. "What's so funny?"

"Laura, you can be as dense as the proverbial forest," Cheryl crowed, shaking her head wonderingly. "This is your wedding night, or don't you remember getting married today, either?"

Stubbornly Laura clung to her shattered pride, her lips forming a mutinous pout. "It's early, yet . . . I'm not tired."

"Good," Jace murmured from above her, reaching for her arm and helping her up. "I don't want you falling asleep on me. After the last couple of months, I think I'd go quietly out of my mind!"

Bidding Cheryl a casual good night wasn't easy, but she managed it. The elevator doors closed abruptly, trapping her inside the confined space, and she trembled as she raised her eyes to the large man beside her. His tall, massive frame seemed to overshadow her for a moment, and she knew her face reflected increasing apprehension.

As she stared at him, Jace's laughter stilled. "Hey, you're really nervous, aren't you?"

"Yes, I'm s-sorry, but I can't seem to . . . to help it," she stammered, lowering her eyes to the pulse throbbing in his neck.

"Good," he said, his voice seeming overloud in the small intimacy of the elevator.

"What?"

"Look," he demanded, holding up his large hand for her inspection. There was a slight tremble in his fingers. "I'm scared too, Laura," he admitted, his voice quiet. "Do you think a fear of failure is a woman's prerogative?"

"But you're always so sure of yourself . . . I never suspected . . ."

"Sometimes a man talks big to cover up his uncertainties. I know I'm a fairly good lover, but don't you understand, it's never mattered to me before. If I'd failed to deliver, it wouldn't have hurt anything but my pride, but with you it's different. I couldn't walk away from you, not ever in this life. The thought of facing you in the morning, knowing I hadn't been able to break through that wall of reserve you've been hiding behind, terrifies me."

Sudden warmth swept through her. He was all male, this man she had married. A man's ego was a sensitive thing, and she realized it had taken a lot of courage to admit his own fears to her. Once again she was disarmed by his sensitivity. It seemed he would do anything to save her feelings, even if it meant exposing his own. Her mind made up, she raised shining eyes to his as they halted outside their door.

"I love you, Jace Matthews!"

"That's what I'm counting on," he groaned.

9

Jace followed close behind her as she entered the hotel room.

"Do you like it?"

"Like it?" she murmured, her eyes surveying the sitting room. "It's lovely."

The walls were painted a beautiful shade of cream. Rose carpeting was plush beneath her feet, and she had the urge to remove her shoes and walk barefoot across the thick surface. A cream-and-rose love seat occupied the center of the room facing the panoramic view from the window, flanked by two comfortable-looking armchairs.

"The bedroom's through there and the bathroom connects to both rooms. I'll be a gentleman and let you have the shower first."

Nodding, she thanked him. "I won't be long," she promised.

True to her promise, Laura's shower took much less time than usual. Wrapping the skimpy hotel bath towel around her, she tucked it securely over her breasts.

Plugging in her blow dryer, she held it while running a brush through the thick strands of her hair.

This task accomplished, Laura unplugged the dryer and returned it to her traveling case. Entering the bedroom, she breathed a sigh of relief to find it empty. Spotting her case beside Jace's larger, more masculine one, she quickly placed it on the bed.

"Oh, no!"

Laura bit her lip in consternation, staring into the suitcase. Her hand reached out and clasped a rumpled-looking note in Cheryl's hand, avoiding the gossamer folds of the lovely peignoir beneath. Cheryl had removed her pajamas in favor of something a little more romantic. The note finished with, "Hope you like your wedding present. Love, Frank and Cheryl."

Extracting the lovely garment with a shaking hand, she couldn't resist holding it against her and turning to the mirrored dresser in the corner. What she saw reflected there caused her to catch her breath in nervous anticipation. It was a fantasy in white, with subtle gold threading running through the lace, and minute tie-string straps at the shoulders. Easy on and easy off, she thought, a blush suffusing her whole body as she slipped it over her head.

She tensed as the sound of the bathroom door opening caught her attention, turning an unseeing gaze toward the window. She heard his footsteps falter briefly as he entered the bedroom. The bathroom light was switched off, she heard the door closing, and her breath seemed permanently caught in her throat as he approached.

Her nostrils picked up the scent of the spicy after-shave Jace favored, and nervous fingers clenched the lacy peignoir closer about her body.

"It's a lovely view, isn't it?" she asked.

Well, it wasn't exactly a lie, she told herself. Even though she had been too preoccupied to see anything, from this height the view must be wonderful.

"Turn around!" Before she had time to think about it, she turned, and she heard the quick intake of his breath.

"Beautiful," he murmured. The caressing quality of his voice drew her, and she raised her eyes to meet the sensual scrutiny of his. Any advantage she thought she might have gained by surprising him with her appearance was quickly lost by her own reaction. Clad only in a knee-length toweling robe, his still-dampened flesh gleamed like burnished mahogany, while the dark hair on his chest drew her fascinated gaze.

Without speaking a word, he removed his robe.

Long moments passed as she studied him. Strangely enough, her initial embarrassment lessened, and then disappeared entirely. No words were needed, and as his eyes moved downward, he didn't try to hide his desire.

It's like moving in a dream, she thought as her garment joined his robe. The femininity she had so long repressed surged within her as she realized the powerful effect her woman's body was having on him. If she had had any doubts about the strength of her own appeal, they were laid to rest as her eyes once again met his, nearly molten with need.

"Come here!"

The whispered command was nearly obliterated by the huskiness of his voice. On shaking legs she covered the distance between them, until she stood within inches of the warmth emanating from his body.

Lightly his lips brushed over her face, never quite settling where she wanted them. He dropped little kisses

132

freely over her tingling flesh, but still he avoided her lips. She was ready to scream in protest. His tongue caressingly traced her mouth, lingering in the corners with frustrating thoroughness, and although she eagerly parted her mouth, he once again moved his head, this time to moisten the delicate hollow of her ear.

"Jace, please . . ." she moaned, twising her head in an attempt to capture the disturbing mouth now nuzzling her throat.

"Love me, honey," he groaned against her pulsing throat.

"I do . . . I do!"

"Then show me."

"I . . . I can't," she protested, her eyes widening as she finally realized what he expected of her. All her earlier fears descended, and she felt inadequate to deal with his demands.

"I could kiss you into submission, Laura, but that's not what I want. My hands and mouth want to hold and taste every inch of you, and I want you to know the joys to be found in the same kind of wanting. I don't need blind submission from you. I want you to know the pleasure of awakening my body to passion, just as I want to discover the delight of arousing yours."

She had never felt as alone as she did at that moment. Jace was making it clear that he wouldn't accept passivity from her. He expected her to initiate their lovemaking, and the knowledge suddenly made her angry. Belatedly, she tried to cover her nakedness.

"You're not being fair!"

"Fair," he exploded, jerking her against his pulsing maleness. "There's no *fair* in making love, Laura. We're equal as soon as we begin the loving, with the same advantages. Your hands will lift me to the same heights that mine will lift you. Why should I settle for less, when I want it all!"

An image of Phillip, using her body until he was satisfied, crossed her mind, and she flinched from the memory. Jace, seeing her recoil, raked a shaking hand through his hair after releasing her, turning to stare out of the window in an attitude of defeat.

Laura barely noticed. She remembered Phillip's bitter recriminations when she couldn't respond to him, the other women, the degradation she had suffered. His own macho image had molded his lovemaking. As a result, she had been left feeling inadequate; any tentative overtures on her part had been quickly suppressed by him, until she had been afraid to show any emotion whatsoever.

A relieved smile crossed her face, and her eyes glowed with the love she felt toward the man who had understood her problems with more insight than she had herself. Jace drew in his breath sharply when her palms slid down his spine, and elated with his response, she allowed them to linger teasingly at the base. Boldly her palms slid around to caress his hips, moving steadily until her hands grasped his knotted stomach muscles. He tried to turn, but her arms stopped him.

"Play fair yourself, honey," he gasped, tilting his head to enable her seeking lips to caress the back of his neck.

"You said there's no fair in making love."

"You're driving me insane!"

Now she knew the fullness of arousal gained by her own actions . . . and she reveled in the knowledge. With renewed zeal her mouth tried to cover every inch of his back, while her hands clutched the hair of his chest.

With a muffled groan he forced her hands to release him long enough for him to turn. Immediately Laura's ascendancy was lost as his hands clutched her hips. Her gasp at the touch of his aroused body was lost under the onslaught of his ravaging kiss.

Her fingers buried themselves in the hair at his nape, holding his mouth locked to hers when he would have lifted his head. His hands moved upward to her waist, one curving around until it cupped her breast, while his thumb rubbed the rosy peak into vibrant life. Tearing her mouth from his, she groaned, drawing the air gratefully into tortured lungs.

When she opened her eyes, his face was a revelation. Hard, chiseled lines were softened miraculously with passion, thick dark lashes fanning luxuriously against his cheeks.

Suddenly those lashes lifted, and a smile like none other she had ever received from him creased his mouth. His smile held passion, yes . . . but also tenderness, love, and . . . gratitude. She felt humbled by his pleasure, and her finger gently traced his cheek.

He bent and effortlessly lifted her in his arms. Walking swiftly, he placed her on the bed, looking down at her briefly before covering her waiting body with his own.

"Now it's my turn," he whispered. With delicate precision his mouth and hands learned her body, moving inexorably until her mind was spinning with sensation. Now any initiation belonged solely to him. Her body was only capable of response, her hands clenching and unclenching on the spread. Suddenly she stiffened, her body exploding, the heat moving upward until it obliterated all conscious thought. She was transported to another world, a world at first frighteningly strange, but soon a place she never wanted to leave.

"There it is, honey . . . there it is," he sighed, a tremor coursing through him as he raised glistening eyes to meet hers. His mouth feathered tiny kisses across her lips, trailing down her neck until it opened hotly over her breast. She could no more prevent the throaty cry of pleasure from escaping her than she could prevent her body from arching against his touch.

As if waiting for the movement, he once again raised his head, watching the conflicting emotions crossing her face avidly.

"Don't look at me like that," she whispered, prevented from turning her head by his hand against her neck.

For long moments Jace held her.

"Do you know how beautiful you look?"

At his huskily voiced question she buried her face in his throat, mumbling a protest.

Tentatively her fingers, unable to keep still, began caressing his back. Again his mouth and hands took over, but she didn't mind at all. She was more than ready to give him the delight he had shown her. His hands clenched on either side of her head as his tongue plundered the eagerly receptive cavern of her mouth. His body sought and found what it was seeking, and his groan was lost within the warmth of her mouth.

He moved slowly at first, but quickly built to a violent rhythm. Her own cry mingled with his, and as she followed his lead, they traveled toward the peak together. They reached her place at almost the same moment, and as they shuddered together within each other's arms, they were no longer two people, but one . . . and it was no longer her place, but theirs.

Laura was awakened by the strident ringing of the telephone beside the bed.

"Hello?"

There was laughter at the other end before a disgustingly bright voice said, "Your evening must have been rather busy for you to sleep until noon!"

Flustered, Laura was unable to reply to Cheryl's teasing with even a semblance of composure. Jace certainly hadn't allowed her much sleep, turning to her again and again in the night. No, that wasn't exactly being fair, she conceded wryly, clutching the sheet tighter across her still-tender breasts. She could recall at least one particular instance when she had boldly initiated a renewal of their lovemaking, just as Jace had been ready to fall asleep. She still shivered when she recalled his pleased chuckles. For an agonizing moment she had thought he was laughing at her, but before she could turn away, the heat of his response had told her how wrong she was. He had guided her in new ways of pleasing him, and she had eagerly followed his instruction. That time had been the very best, she remembered, feeling her breathing quicken as varying images teased her mind.

"Hey, are you going back to sleep?"

"What? Oh, sorry, Cheryl."

"I should hope you are," she teased, finally getting around to explaining the reason for her call. Before Laura could tell Cheryl they would meet her and Frank for lunch, the receiver was taken from her hand.

"Cheryl, good morning!"

To her consternation, Jace threw back his head and

roared with laughter. "Mmmm, it was a good night," he murmured, wicked lights dancing in his eyes as he studied the indignant figure beside him.

"All right, we'll meet you in the restaurant in half an hour. Yes, why don't you and Frank order something for us. I want to leave for home by two o'clock. That'll give me time to check out and load up the car without my woman fainting from hunger in the meantime. Thanks!"

When he referred to her as his woman in that caressing way, any anger Laura had been harboring at the high-handedness of his actions disappeared.

Much to her disgust, she suffered a recurrence of shyness when he replaced the receiver, leaning over her to do so. Avoiding his eyes, she wasn't ready when he quickly tugged at the sheet, stripping the covering to her waist.

"Jace, we'll have to hurry . . . don't!"

"There's plenty of time," he grinned. "If we shower together, we'll save at least fifteen minutes."

His hands moved caressingly over her supple flesh, and she found herself mindlessly responding. A long, long time later she lay in his arms, a small satisfied smile tugging the corners of her moistened lips.

"We'd better get up. You can have the shower first."

"We'll share, there's plenty of room," he mumbled against her throat.

"If we share, we never will get around to eating lunch." She laughed, tugging at his hair in an attempt to still his wandering mouth. "And since I didn't have any break-fast, I'm starving," she complained.

With a pained grunt he lifted his head, shaking it ruefully. "Woman, you've got no romance in your soul!"

"No?" she whispered doubtfully, allowing her hand to travel intimately down his body.

"All right, I take it back," he gasped, a shudder rippling through his large frame. "To hell with lunch. We'll grab a hamburger on the drive back," he sighed, once more reaching for her.

Before his large hands could seduce her, she leaped from the bed, giggling as he lunged for her. From the comparative safety of the bathroom doorway she turned, her giggling increasing when she saw him still struggling to extricate himself from the tangled bedding. "Since you're so slow this morning, I'll have my shower first."

Laura felt surprised, and a little regretful, when he didn't join her as he'd threatened. She felt she had never been so alive before, or so eager to begin a new day. Finishing quickly, she stepped out, drying herself haphazardly and brushing her teeth in record time.

Leaving the bathroom with the towel wrapped around her, she stopped in amazement. There was Jace, sprawled facedown on the bed, sound asleep. At this rate she wasn't ever going to get a meal, she thought.

Indignantly she marched over to him, pulling back the covers in one fell swoop. She was never sure of what happened next. One minute she was gripping his shoulder, and the next she was lying beneath him!

He began tickling her until her laughter brought tears.

"Tell me you're sorry," he demanded, grinning at her discomfort without mercy.

"I . . . I'm sorry," she gasped.

"Admit who's boss!"

Laughing even harder, she cried, "I admit I'm the . . . the boss."

At once his hands renewed the attack. He was strad-
dling her body, holding her hands over her head in one
of his.

Finally she couldn't stand it any longer, and she
giggled her answer.

"I didn't hear you!"

"You're the boss, you beast!"

His mouth covered hers, and the laughter was choked
off abruptly. His tongue found and played with hers, and
before she had a chance to think rationally, her mouth
was answering his. With stunned surprise she felt his
eager hardness pressing against her, and immediately
twisted her body in an attempt to gain a closer contact.

He shifted and she lay pliant, thinking he meant to
begin their lovemaking in earnest, only to stare in
stunned surprise when he rose to his feet. Stretching his
arms over his head, totally unembarrassed as he stood in
front of her in all his male glory, he slanted her a grin.

"I hope you left plenty of hot water!"

"You . . . you . . ."

The pillow missed him by inches, hitting the bathroom
door with a muffled thud. She heard him whistling as he
adjusted the water. He certainly sounded happy—the
typical avenging male. Well, he had certainly paid her
back in her own coin!

For comfort during the trip back home, Laura chose to
wear a silky white pullover top shaped like a sweat shirt,
with ribbed trim at the waist and sleeves. Coupled with
gray cotton velveteen pants, the outfit was elegant
enough to mark the occasion, yet functionally comfortable.

Brushing her long hair into a semblance of order, she

left it loose as Jace liked it. She used a minimum of makeup before turning to pack her bags. Deciding to be generous, she quickly folded Jace's clothing and packed it in his larger case. She assumed the items on the bed were what he'd chosen to wear today, and she found herself agreeing with his taste. With his eyes he would look terrific in the casual Western-cut shirt in blue and gray, outlined in bold black stitching—but then, he looked good in anything.

Jace caught her with a silly grin on her face, and she flushed when he quirked one bold eyebrow upward. "Penny for them?"

"They're not worth it," she grumbled, bending to fasten the straps on his suitcase.

"Hey, you forgot my robe."

"Well, give it to me, then," she muttered.

This left him as God had intended, and she quickly looked away while he laughingly began dressing.

While he took their bags to the car, she walked into the busy restaurant, almost despairing of finding Cheryl and Frank in the crush of people. She needn't have worried, for they were sitting close to the entrance and waved her over. After the first few moments of initial shyness, not helped much by her friends' teasing comments regarding her glowing appearance, Laura found herself relaxing.

The meal was informal as well as restful, and she enjoyed it thoroughly. The four of them were surprisingly comfortable with each other, and she marveled at how quickly Jace had fit in with her friends. Although she was looking forward to the trip home, and the beginning of her life with Jace, she was almost sorry when Cheryl and Frank walked them to their car.

"We'll see you two later, then. Have a safe trip home," Cheryl said, hugging Laura before turning to Jace. "You take care of her or you'll answer to me!" With a mocking grin Jace grabbed her, looking to Frank for permission before lowering his head. Cheryl's cheeks were flushed when Jace finally released her.

Laura couldn't believe the stab of jealous emotion which pierced her at the sight of another woman in Jace's arms, even though it was only Cheryl. She realized it made no difference—she didn't want him ever to hold anyone but her. The smile she gave Cheryl was over-bright, and by the gleam in Cheryl's eyes, it didn't fool the other girl one little bit.

"Laura, if you don't take care of *him,* you're out of your mind!"

"Hmmm, so much for loyalty," Laura retorted, turning from her friend with a toss of her head.

"Jace, she's jealous," Cheryl cried, a bubble of laughter escaping her rosy lips. "You're going to have to be careful."

"She won't have any cause for complaint," Jace murmured, pulling Laura against his side with a caressing hand.

She sat close beside Jace during the drive, enjoying the scenery and finding herself completely relaxed now in his company. The sky rejoiced with her in her happiness. The sun glowed down brilliantly upon the verdant landscape, causing the rushing river, which appeared occasionally, to sparkle in foam-flecked splendor.

How was it possible, in such a short space of time, to find her whole existence tied irrevocably to the man sitting so comfortingly beside her? she mused. At that moment he turned his head and gave her a slow smile, and she felt an inexorable rise of emotion. As the car traveled the miles, her mind whirled with future possibilities, and almost before she was aware of it, she blurted her thoughts aloud. "Jace, do you like children?"

Her cheeks burned when he burst into laughter, and she avoided his eyes, trying to fight down tears. Concentrating almost desperately on the scenery in an attempt to hide her hurt, she noticed with a sense of unreality that they were already driving past Sacramento.

"Hey, what's wrong?"

"I didn't think my question was all that funny!"

She could have died when her voice broke on the last word, and she lowered her eyes, biting her lip.

"If you remember, we'd just been talking of what we'd like to do together, that's why I laughed when you mentioned children," he explained, drawing her against him until he was close enough to nuzzle his mouth against her ear. "I'll wait to teach you skiing if you'd prefer having a baby right away. I would rather make babies with you, anyway," he teased.

Hope burgeoned inside of her at his words. She wanted to have children as soon as possible, but the decision couldn't be hers alone. Her voice held a lingering doubt when she turned to speak to him. "Are you sure?"

"Honey, I'm forty, or near enough for it not to matter. I want to be young enough to enjoy a family, and I would prefer you to have them while it's safe for you to do so."

"You're not just saying that because you know I want them?"

"If I hadn't been thinking along those lines, sweetheart," he murmured, a wry twist to his mobile lips, "I'd have used some form of precaution last night. You do realize you might already be carrying my child?"

"Do you think so?"

He laughed at the suddenly starry-eyed expression in her eyes, and this time she joined him.

Before their trip, Laura had gone to her new home with Jace while he packed. She hadn't gathered anything but vague impressions on that occasion, but now, as Jace took her on a guided tour, she realized that decor was another thing on which they seemed to agree.

The living room with its modern lighting, Formica-topped tables, and built-in banquettes was contemporary, but far from stark. The large open space was comfortably furnished, and the antique Oriental rugs, brown leather-covered sofas and chairs, and rock-walled fireplace gave a feeling of coziness to the large room.

The second floor was virtually empty of furniture, and Jace suggested making it into temporary guest rooms until the children were old enough to be transferred upstairs. At this she flushed, seeing the four bedrooms and adjoining baths with new eyes.

Although the dining area, painted a darker color than the rest of the open living space, to exaggerate its separateness, delighted her, as did the kitchen, spacious enough to house a center island with grill-range and cook-top and a built-in home office flooded with light from a skylight overhead, it was their bedroom which she loved most.

Furnished in amethyst and gray, it was a cool, soothing retreat from the rich earth tones found in the other rooms. The furniture was placed at an angle for interest and included a built-in platform that doubled as a headboard. She walked around the room in silence. Opening the walk-in closet, large enough to be used as a small storeroom, she felt a jolt when she noticed her own clothes, brought over while they were gone by his secretary, hanging opposite Jace's.

"I feel as if I've lived here always," she whispered.

His arms came around her, holding her tightly against the warmth of his body. "I must have had you in mind when I designed and furnished it, then . . . because you fit inside perfectly."

"Don't you think you should call your parents?" he questioned her several minutes later, while helping with the unpacking.

"Should I ask them over?"

She couldn't wait for her mother to see the house, and she couldn't hide that eagerness from her perceptive husband.

"Why don't you invite them for dinner if they haven't already eaten?"

Checking her watch, she shook her head with a sense of real regret. "No, Emma always serves dinner at six, unless they're expecting company, and it's already half-past."

"Now that you mention it, my stomach certainly feels half-past!"

"In that case, I'll leave you to finish the unpacking while I go make that phone call."

"Hey, that's not fair. Come back here and do your share, woman!"

"You come out to the kitchen and help with dinner," she retorted.

"You win!" He grinned, raising his hands in defeat, and Laura left the room with an answering smile on her face.

10

Even though he had acted horrified at her suggestion that he help with their meal, Laura felt his arms around her waist not many minutes later.

"Mmmm, smells good."

"Since it's only canned soup, that's not much of a compliment, and anyway, you can't smell with your nose buried in my hair."

"I didn't say what it was that smells good, woman," he teased, nuzzling his mouth against her ear.

"Since you appear to have so much excess energy, you can fix the salad."

"Your wish is my command!"

Watching the deft movements of his hands as he fixed the greens decoratively, she grimaced. "You made me think you weren't any use in a kitchen."

"You assumed I was useless, honey. How do you think I got to be this size without eating?"

"I guessed you had somebody come in to fix your meals, or else you ate out," she admitted, spooning the hot soup carefully into bowls. "You're probably a better cook than I am. I always did my share, but I'm not as imaginative as Cheryl."

"I didn't marry you for your prowess in the kitchen," he murmured, laughing when her cheeks assumed a rosy hue.

Placing their meal on a tray and carrying it through to the dining room, she retorted, "You didn't marry me for my prowess anywhere else, either!"

As Jace sat beside her with assumed meekness, she determinedly spooned soup into her mouth, trying without much success not to let his teasing bother her. His next remark caused her carefully feigned facade to crumble when she choked on her soup.

"How do you know I didn't guess at your potential? You didn't do too badly last night!"

Their light meal didn't take long to finish, and while Jace went to prepare a fire, she made short work of the dishes.

Later, entering the bedroom, she searched in the closet for a change of clothing. She wanted something to match her mood, and without too much searching found the very thing. She had chosen it during her buying spree with Cheryl, and up until now hadn't had the courage to wear it. With her hair it was rather daring, but strangely enough the color tones were superb, she decided, holding it against herself and studying her mirrored reflection. It was an evening chemise with yards of bright pink silk touched with aqua and wine in a perfect soft pullover dress cinched by a double-wrapping belt. With her dainty flat sandals it would be perfect for her reunion with her parents tonight!

Rushing through her shower seemed almost criminal in

the luxurious confines of the large bathroom, but she managed it in record time. While she dried herself with the fluffy bath towel hanging on a warming rack, she looked longingly toward the sunken tub, eyes widening in anticipation when she noticed spa fittings in the blue-gray tile.

The sound of the doorbell interrupted her thoughts. She could hear her mother's excited tones mingling with Jace's deeper ones. Hurrying through her dressing and running a quick brush through her hair, she quickly left the room.

Stopping in the hallway to adjust a slipping heel strap, she smiled, making an effort to control her excitement. Regaining her lost poise, she quietly stepped through into the living room. Her father's hand was clasped to Jace's shoulder, a beaming grin on his face.

"Laura, we didn't see you standing there," her mother cried, coming forward and enfolding her daughter in her arms. "Oh, darling. Your father and I are so happy for you both. The two of you were meant for each other."

Allowing herself to be drawn forward, Laura accepted her father's kiss.

"You couldn't have chosen a husband who pleased me more, Laura," he said, smiling at her with rare approval.

Laura couldn't help her mouth from curling in a cynical travesty of a smile. She knew by the sudden frown on his face that Jace had noticed. To cover the rather strained moment, she turned to her mother, hoping her face wasn't as tense as she feared. "Come on. I'll show you the rest of the house."

While she took Irene on a guided tour, Laura silently fumed. Jace and Darryl had headed for the bar, and they weren't even out of sight before her father was talking business. With concern she noticed the lines of bitterness creasing her mother's eyes and mouth—even more apparent than the last time they had been together.

Irene was making an effort to appear relaxed, but Laura wasn't fooled. Once in the bedroom, she turned to her mother, who was absently admiring an impressionistic painting adorning the wall above the bed.

"Do you want to talk about Father?"

Irene shook her head. "What is there to say, darling?" she muttered, crossing her arms and clutching her elbows with trembling fingers. "Nothing's changed since the last time we talked. If anything, the situation's worsened. Now he doesn't even bother thinking up excuses, but just informs me which nights he'll be away from home."

Their eyes met across the width of the room, and as if a dam had burst, Irene's composure cracked. While dry sobs racked Irene's body, Laura offered what comfort she could, leading her mother toward the bed and helping her lie down.

"Don't torture yourself this way. There has to be some sane, rational explanation for Father's behavior. I'm sure he'll confide in you sooner or later."

This last was said through gritted teeth. She wanted to scream, drive her clenched firsts into the wall—do anything to erase the hopeless misery from her mother's face. Her own emotions felt ravaged, unable to withstand the deterioration in her mother's character.

"I'm going to get you a brandy," she whispered, brushing a stray wisp of hair from Irene's cheek.

With almost inhuman strength Irene clutched at her hand, a look of terror distorting her features. "Promise me you'll say nothing to Darryl, Laura."

"But, Mother—"

"Why do you think I can't bring myself to question him?" she cried bitterly. "Don't you understand? I live in fear of hearing the truth, because it might be the beginning of the end for our marriage. I don't want to hear him admit there's another woman. I don't think I could stand it!"

With a pitying sigh Laura pulled her hand from the tensely gripping fingers, lifting it to pat Irene's shoulder consolingly.

"Don't worry," she muttered. "I won't say anything."

Heading for the bar, she was relieved to hear voices coming from the direction of the patio. She poured the golden liquid into a balloon glass in grim-lipped silence, her mind on her father's perfidy. How could he do this to the woman who had loved him devotedly for all these years . . . whose very personality had been stunted at the altar of his monumental selfishness?

Adding ice to the glass, Laura turned to retrace her steps. She had to pass within a few feet of the open patio doors, and as a whisper of subdued conversation reached her ears, she stood rooted to the floor in horrified disbelief.

". . . isn't right. She . . . to be told. I . . . should tell her, Darryl, before she guesses." Laura moved closer, straining now to hear the disjointed words. "I know it's going to be difficult . . . but these things must be faced. It isn't your fault this has happened, and I just don't know how long I can continue covering for you!"

It was Jace's voice, the tones harshly accusing, and she felt the rise of nausea when she heard him admitting to helping her father deceive his wife. Jace was in on her father's deception up to his neck, she thought, bitterness rising violently inside of her. All this time he had been keeping quiet in an attempt to protect his friend. Remembering the broken shell of the once-proud woman that she had left grieving only a few rooms away, Laura felt cold with fury. Any man who could lower himself to be a party to a man deceiving his wife in such a vile manner was himself despicable.

If he could justify her father's actions, wasn't he also capable of eventually discarding his own wife in favor of another woman? Remembering the luscious Marianna, she flinched. Unknown to her, her own expression became the mirror image of her mother's. With a shudder she couldn't suppress, she wondered how long it would be before it was her turn to lie in that bedroom staring at the ceiling with hollow eyes.

A muffled cry escaped her as her nightmare imaginings gained ascendancy. At the sound, Jace, nearest to the open doorway, spun around. For endless moments she allowed all the loathing she felt for him to show on her face, before turning on her heel and returning to her mother.

Barely half an hour later, Irene insisted on bathing her face and rejoining the men. The tension between the four of them was almost tangible, and Laura wasn't a bit surprised when Darryl made the first move to depart. He's probably afraid I'll tell him what I think of him, she thought cynically.

As she watched her parents leave, a feeling of impotent rage engulfed her, and she whirled around to confront the Judas beside her.

"Just what's going on?" The words were hissed between clenched teeth, while her eyes glowed with green fury. "Mother's in a terrible state," she continued, glaring at him with suspicion. "I tried to tell her she was wrong about Father. Until hearing the two of you plotting your deceit, I even believed my own words."

Jace's hands tightened convulsively on her shoulders for a brief moment before he released her. She watched as he moved across the room. He was staring into the distance when he spoke, and Laura almost missed the softly spoken words.

"Your mother's guessed, then?"

"About the other woman?" Laura felt that her bitterness at Jace's deceit would choke her, but she went doggedly on. "Mother's not stupid. Of course she's guessed. In fact, his mistress had the gall to call him at home, and Mother spoke to her. Somehow I never thought you'd stoop to helping a man deceive his wife, Jace. Men should stick together, is that it? Or maybe there's a little something in it for you? I suppose it would be natural, with the debt of gratitude he owes you, for my father to cover up your little indiscretions when the time comes!"

If she had been in any doubt as to his guilt, the low snarl of fury he emitted as he reached for her would have been conviction enough.

"I don't care what you think of me, Laura," he said, jerking her against him, "but I won't stand by while you denigrate your own father, do you understand me?"

Laura stood immobile under his attack, staring at him with dilated eyes until he smothered an oath and released her. Only then, when the warmth of his flesh no longer burned an imprint on her skin, did she find the courage to continue.

"What a fool you must have thought me," she remarked in what was almost a conversational tone. "I made it very easy for you, didn't I, Jace?"

"Laura, it isn't what you're thinking," he replied, taking a step toward her. "Give me a little time, and I'll explain everything to you. I've given my word, but—"

"I'm only thinking what a clever husband I've got, *darling*. No wonder you're my father's fair-haired boy—you're two of a kind."

"Dammit, Laura," he cursed, leaping flames lending false warmth to otherwise cool gray eyes. "You don't have the least little bit of trust in me, do you?"

"I trusted you when I married you," she said, wrapping her arms defensively around her body. "I never suspected you had such an unpleasant side to your character, but now I know better. There has to be respect for there to be trust . . . and I have neither for either you or my father!"

Jace gave her a look of utter disgust before turning to rake a hand through his hair in a tired motion.

"You're behaving like a child!"

"Am I?" She heard the sneer in her voice with a sense of shock, a shock which deepened when, with a snarled imprecation, Jace whirled and pulled her into his arms.

"What happened to the woman I held last night, Laura?" Jace's muttered words words fell on deaf ears as Laura struggled against the insidious warmth of his clasp. She had to fight not only him but also the clamorings of her own body, which remembered only too well the heights she had risen to in the night.

Moistening dry lips with the tip of her tongue, she pulled free, turning in the direction of the bedroom. She just couldn't stand any more tonight. Time enough tomorrow to decide what she was going to do next. She was too tired to think about it right now, she thought.

"Where are you going?"

She spun at the savage inflection in his voice, staring at him nervously. "I'm t-tired," she stammered, forcing herself not to back away from his approach. "I'm going to bed."

Was it her imagination, or did he seem relieved? Since his face hardened again almost immediately, she couldn't be sure she hadn't imagined it.

"I'll be in shortly," he said, a new determination in his voice.

"If you think I'm sharing the bed with you as if nothing's happened, you can forget it," she cried, incensed by his callousness.

"You're my wife," he snarled, grasping her arms in a painful grip and administering a slight shake. "You'll share my bed tonight, and every other night. Do I make myself clear?"

Goaded beyond endurance, she jerked out of his clasp, her eyes full of wild rejection as she met his glance. "I'm going home tomorrow, and there's nothing you can do about it!"

"Running away, Laura? That's your answer to all your problems, isn't it? You just run away from them. But marriage is a serious commitment. You're my wife, and you can't run away from that fact. If you leave, I'll bring you back—don't be in any doubt about that, Laura. I'm not a man to be crossed or made to look an idiot, so don't attempt it."

"That's all you care about, your macho image." She laughed bitterly. "How people would conjecture about the reasons I'd left you so soon," she taunted, her head thrown back defiantly. "Afraid they might think you weren't man enough to satisfy me?"

She had gone too far, she realized, watching his anger

turn to rage. Although she attempted a retreat, it was much too late. This kiss was a travesty of what had gone before, and she nearly crumpled under the onslaught.

Hard hands grasped the elastic neckline of her chemise and ripped it to her waist before returning to cup her breasts with implacable intent. As if the feel of her flesh was enough to arouse him, she heard Jace growl low in his throat, and the sound spread a new kind of terror through her.

Where before his hands had been forceful, now they became gentle on her heated skin, and his mouth opened wider on the bruised softness of hers, his tongue beginning a slow, rotating movement which she was finding it impossible to ignore.

Fresh torment surged through her as she felt her body's betraying response, and she couldn't prevent uttering a tiny moan of arousal. To her everlasting shame, Jace chose that moment to stand back and pull her dress up across her throbbing breasts.

"That display was in the nature of a salutary lesson, sweetheart," he mocked. "Even though you say you hate me, I've taught your body something quite different. But you were right about one thing, I'm not going to make love to you tonight. I'll sleep on the couch. A woman who convicts without letting me utter a word of appeal in my defense is less than attractive."

With shaking legs she crossed the room, never once looking back to where he was standing. She had made a complete and utter fool of herself, and wanted only to lick her wounds in private.

She must have slept from sheer emotional exhaustion, because when she next opened her eyes it was morning.

It didn't take her long to shower and change into pleated wide-wale-corduroy culottes in beige cotton, with a belted sweater over the textured gray crewneck accentuating the smallness of her waist. Knit tights and low boots completed the outfit, and as she put her hair up in a casual topknot, she felt amazed that she could still feel cold under all that clothing.

It took real courage to go in search of Jace, but setting her mouth firmly, she accomplished it, supported by her inner determination. He was seated at the dining table, the remains of his breakfast in front of him, his head buried in the morning paper.

"Good morning," she ventured, walking through into the kitchen before he could reply. Taking a cup off the wall rack, she poured herself some coffee, savoring the familiar aroma as the steam rose in the air.

At the first reviving sip of the hot beverage, she was suddenly appalled by the immaturity of her behavior. She was hiding in the kitchen like a child afraid of punishment, and she wouldn't have it! Uttering a short, unamused laugh, she boldly walked through into the dining room, seating herself beside Jace with every intention of bringing up the painful subject that was on both their minds.

"I'll drive you to work, since your car's still at the apartment." His coolly impersonal tone froze the conciliatory words she'd been about to utter.

"Oh, you needn't bother," she replied, her voice as coolly polite as his. "I can take a bus to the BART station."

"It's no bother," he remarked, leaning back in his chair.

That's it . . . subject closed, she thought. Resentment rose hotly at his callous indifference.

"Jace, I don't know if this marriage is going to work," she said, raising her head and looking into his eyes with a desperate hope that he would contradict her. "How can I possibly trust you after what I found out last night? I won't let you do to me what Father's doing to my mother!"

"When are you going to stop running, Laura? You're my wife, and I don't intend altering that either now or in the future. I think we have something pretty special between us, but a good marriage doesn't just happen. You have to work at it."

"The way my mother worked at hers?" she retorted. "By giving up everything except the whims of your husband? By molding your personality to fit one man's image of the perfect wife, until all sense of individuality and even your pride is gone? No thanks, Jace, I'd stifle in that kind of a marriage, and that seems to be the only kind you can offer."

His lip curled in mocking derision as he rose to his feet, to stand towering above her. "I think you're blowing this way out of proportion. Contrary to your petty accusations, my major concern in keeping your father's confidence was for your mother."

"I wouldn't believe you if you swore on the Bible," she fumed, her anger increasing when he turned his back with a negligent shrug of his shoulders.

"Look, you're going to be late for work as it is. Let's continue this discussion in the car," he suggested with a nonchalance more appropriate to a conversation about the weather than one involving the future of their marriage. Barely controlling her temper, she gathered up her things and marched out to the car in silent fury.

"Laura," he began in a reasonable tone, as they started out of the garage, "let's talk this over sensibly. You haven't even given me a chance to explain my side of this. What kind of love or loyalty does that show? You're trying to make me into a monster, but it just isn't true. I'm not asking anything from you that I wouldn't be willing to give myself. I don't expect blind faith, just a little trust. Do you honestly believe I would have an affair with another woman when I could be making love to you?"

"That's not the point," she blurted out, feeling angry tears well up in her eyes no matter how hard she tried to keep them at bay. "Maybe you wouldn't now, but what about in a year, or five years? The fact that you condone my father's cheating tells me that sooner or later one woman just isn't going to be enough for you!"

Jace's reasonable manner disappeared at her heated accusation, and his mouth thinned to a grim line. "I'm not about to indulge in a mud-slinging contest with you. If you can't discuss this like a mature adult, we'd better put off talking about the problem until you're calm enough to see sense. In the meantime, I think it might be best if we do as you suggested last night—maintain separate sleeping quarters. I don't relish the idea of making love to a temperamental child."

Laura couldn't believe her ears! Was he using the cessation of their physical relationship as a threat? Did he think he could bring her into line by denying her his bed? The arrogance of the man was unbelievable.

"That'll be just fine with me," she snapped, hurt more than she cared to admit by his apparent indifference to whether she slept in his bed or not. She almost hated him for renewing her old lack of confidence in herself as a woman. If he cared so little for her lovemaking, he would get his wish, she vowed. She would show him how little she cared for his company!

She breathed a relieved sigh when her office building came into sight. Pulling over to the curb with an economy of movement she envied, he turned to face her, one arm leaning negligently upon the steering wheel.

Flushing, she quickly opened the door and got out, hoping the unsteadiness of her legs wasn't visible.

"I'll have your car brought around later today," he promised, his perceptive gaze narrowing on her scarlet cheeks.

By this time she wanted only to escape from his overpowering presence, and was almost ready to promise him anything. "All right," she said, closing the door with a slam and quickly walking into the building.

The furor over her sudden marriage was all she had expected, and when she finally entered her office she felt wilted from the effort it cost to play the blushing bride. Throwing herself into her work provided the panacea she desperately needed, and it was with a sense of irritation that she raised her head when Josie knocked on her door.

"Maria Cabral's outside," Josie remarked, motioning behind her. Looking past the other woman, Laura frowned at the sight of a clearly distraught Maria, her face pale as she stared nervously around her at the activity in the outer office.

"Show her in, Josie," she said, looking into the other woman's concerned face. "She looks shattered. I wonder what's happened."

"You won't know until she tells you," Josie replied briskly, turning in the doorway.

Laura smiled, knowing Josie's caustic comment was an attempt to cover her own concern. Games, games—everybody plays games, she thought sadly.

"Maria, it's good to see you." Laura smiled gently, getting to her feet and helping the other woman into a chair. Seating herself beside Maria, she asked, "What's the trouble?"

As if her innocent question had released the control Maria was holding on her emotions, tears began to pour silently down her cheeks. Without another word Laura closed the door, pulling mud-brown curtains across the glassed-in portions in an attempt to provide Maria with necessary privacy.

Handing Maria several tissues from the box on her desk, she leaned forward. She didn't have long to wait, and as Maria's words poured forth, she stiffened. Apparently Miguel was attempting to work two full-time jobs, since he couldn't make enough money otherwise. What caused Laura to stare at Maria with appalled horror were the tiny capsules in the older woman's palm.

"Where did you find these?"

Even to her own ears her words sounded hoarse, and she couldn't seem to tear her eyes away from the drugs, so small, so lethal . . . so capable of turning a healthy boy like Miguel into a zombie.

"I find when I clean my Miguel's room," Maria sobbed. "He wrap in paper and hide."

Without thinking, Laura put her hand out, and Maria placed the pills in her palm. With a violent movement Laura dumped them in the wastebasket. Getting to her feet, she left the office, walking over to Josie's desk.

"Do you have an extra coffeecup?"

"Sure, bottom drawer," Josie replied. "What's up?"

"Maria found some uppers in Miguel's room," she whispered.

Josie's face creased into a sad grimace. "The pattern's always the same, isn't it?"

Straightening from her crouched position beside Josie's desk, Laura looked at the earthenware mug in her hands with unseeing eyes. "Josie, what in God's name can I do? What can I tell Maria?"

At her anguished words, Josie frowned furiously, taking the cup from Laura's shaking hands and filling it with coffee. "Now, you listen here," she demanded, putting the steaming coffee on the desk. "You've done all you can for Miguel, and you'll continue to do so. That's all you can ask of yourself. The rest is up to him. When you start blaming yourself for the mess other people make of their lives, then it's time to find another line of work. You just can't let yourself feel it personally, or you'll end up needing tranquilizers yourself."

"Hello, honey."

Swiveling around at the sound of the deep voice, she caught her breath in a gasp. Jace's presence here, in the place she had expected to be totally free of him, unnerved her. Mumbling an introduction, she almost laughed at the awed admiration on Josie's face—almost, but not quite.

"What are you doing here?"

"I brought your car around," he replied, turning to face her after giving Josie a smile. "I thought I'd take you to lunch."

"I'm afraid lunch is out," she said, motioning with her

head to Maria's huddled figure, clearly visible through the open door. Seeing the frown quickly darkening his brow, she hurried to explain, not wanting his anger to erupt in front of Josie.

"What you're telling me, then, is that the son of the woman in your office is using drugs to enable him to work long enough hours to support his family . . . right?"

"Yes," Laura admitted. "Don't get the wrong idea, though. Miguel's a good boy, with a good brain. He wouldn't deliberately cause his mother grief!"

Laura was prevented from further speech by Jace's departure. Both she and Josie stared in openmouthed surprise as his quick, pantherish strides took him across the room to her office.

"Well!"

Josie's exclamation echoed Laura's own thoughts at Jace's high-handed actions. Really, it isn't enough that he tries to control my private life, now he's sticking his nose in at work too, she thought.

"Now, Laura," Josie soothed. "Don't look like that!"

"I don't know what you're talking about," she replied, her face mutinous.

"You've married quite a man, honey," Josie said, nodding her head sagely. "You're not going to get the upper hand with that one. He's just what you need."

Before Laura had a chance to utter the scathing comment burning her tongue, the door to her office opened. Her eyes widened at the sight of Jace with his arm around Maria's shoulders, but it was the other woman's face that left her speechless. It was as if the years of worry and care had been wiped away, leaving Maria looking almost young again. The reason for this was obvious when Jace turned to Maria with a winning smile, admonishing her gently, "You tell him to be there, that he has a job with me if he wants it."

"I will tell him, señor," she promised, looking adoringly into Jace's miraculously softened face. *"Vaya con Dios."*

"Go with God," he said in return, turning to face a silent Laura after Maria departed.

Unable to face his scrutiny, Laura turned to Josie, only to wish she hadn't. Josie was staring from the outer door to Jace, a bemused expression on her lined face.

"I can't begin to tell you what a miracle you've wrought." Josie's expression was intent as she shook her head in disbelief. "We've watched Maria aging before our eyes over the years, but she walked out of here with steps as light as a young girl's."

"Everyone needs someone," he replied understandingly, his eyes drifting meaningfully toward Laura. "Miguel will be trained in a job with a future, and if there are any problems, Maria's to let me know. If the boy proves to be as bright as you say, I may make other arrangements for the furtherance of his education. If that happens, he will of course still receive his full salary."

"Why?" Her lips felt stiff as she whispered the question.

"Because Maria loves her son," he remarked quietly. With dawning comprehension Laura stared at him, remembering what he had told her about his own childhood without the mother who might have loved him. Maria loved her son, as he himself would have liked to have been loved . . . and he wouldn't see her suffer because of it. He hadn't been able to prevent his own birth causing his mother's early death, but he could prevent Maria from killing herself with worry over Miguel.

There was a goodness inside of Jace she had only guessed at until this moment. It seemed impossible that he could be so kind and considerate with Maria, and yet so immoral in his dealings with other women. For the first time since the night before, she wondered if she had perhaps misjudged him. More than anything, she wanted to clear up the misunderstanding between them, but after all the angry words, she didn't know how to go about it. Her pride wouldn't allow her to be the first to broach the subject.

"Shall we go?" she asked.

His lowered lids hooded his eyes, but she could tell he was angry at her cool response by the sudden tightening of his mobile mouth.

"That was my intention all along, honey," he murmured, a derisive slant twisting his lips.

11

~~~~~~~~~~

Laura, wait up!"

"What are you doing here at this hour of the morning?" Laura asked as Cheryl swung into stride beside her. "You're supposed to be on leave to prepare for your wedding, not to gad around town," Laura teased while the elevator carried them upward.

"Believe it or not, there's nothing left for me to do until Sunday, when I say 'I do'!"

Stepping out of the elevator and automatically looking through her shoulder bag for the office keys, Laura paused to give her friend a disbelieving look. "You're never that organized. I don't believe it!"

A sheepish look crossed Cheryl's expressive face. "Well, to be honest, my mother kicked me out for the day. She said my dithering was getting on her nerves."

Laura laughed. "Now *that* I believe!"

Weaving between desks with Cheryl at her heels, Laura replied to the various greetings sent her way, with her mind only partially on her co-workers. It was almost like running a gauntlet, she thought, as she reached the door to her office. They were still teasing her about her marriage, but for her the jokes were wearing a little thin, especially since the emotional freeze between her and Jace had not thawed at all in the last three days.

While Cheryl chatted to Josie for a few minutes, Laura sorted through her mail, trying to deny the feelings of unhappiness that plagued her. If only Jace would make the first move, she would gladly listen to his explanations now. If his suggestion that they maintain separate bedrooms had been calculated to break down her resistance, it was turning out to be devastatingly successful. Those moments of ecstasy in his arms on their wedding night returned to haunt her more powerfully than she would have believed possible as she lay lonely and sleepless on the cot in the upstairs guest room. The last few nights had been sheer torture, and she had longed for Jace to come to her, to make any overture that would signal his desire to end their three-day-long cold war.

When Cheryl rejoined her, they chatted briefly about the wedding rehearsal that was to take place the following evening. The more she talked, the more nervous Cheryl became, and Laura didn't have to wonder why Cheryl's mother preferred her daughter out of the house for a few hours. The bride-to-be had such a case of prewedding jitters, she was enough to drive anyone batty.

Convincing Cheryl that there was probably something her mother desperately needed her for at home, she finally managed to finish going through the mail. If only her other problems could be solved so easily!

"Ready for a night on the town?" Jace had returned from work that evening in obviously high spirits, and his good mood was doing nothing for Laura's already frayed nerves. The rapidly deteriorating situation between them seemed to affect him not at all.

"I'd rather not," she said, turning away to hide the distress in her eyes. "I've had an exhausting day at work and I was really looking forward to a nice hot bath and a good book."

"That's a lame excuse, and you know it," he mocked, turning her to face him. "Why do you continue with this attitude?"

"Attitude?" she spluttered, trying in vain to wrench herself free of his grasp. "It's your attitude that amazes me. How can you go on pretending that nothing's wrong, when we've hardly spoken during the last three days and you've been out till all hours every night? It just goes to prove what I suspected—that you're all too happy to find your pleasures elsewhere, especially when the little woman won't jump to gratify your every whim!" Her voice was bitter and harsh with jealousy when she added, "Just to satisfy my curiosity, Jace, where *have* you been? With Marianna?"

"No!" He almost shouted the word. "I've been working late, but I don't expect you to believe that. Lately it seems like you can't believe anything I say." Laura raised her eyes to his, surprised at the note of genuine pain in his voice. "Please, Laura," he asked in a calmer tone, "can't we call a truce for now, take these next couple days to cool down before we try to decide our future? I'm doing everything in my power to make this marriage work. Is a few days' grace period asking too much? After that, I promise I'll explain everything."

Jace was right—of course he was! She could feel the warmth of his hands burning through her clothes to her skin, making her vibrantly aware of the male smell of him, the exciting closeness of his body. She was no longer struggling against his hold, and as her anger abated, familiar and even more dangerous emotions were making themselves felt.

She couldn't stop the momentum of her body as he pulled her closer to his warmth. Their mouths met, clung briefly, and then separated. Smiling shyly, she asked, "Where do you want to go?"

As Laura awoke the next morning, she remembered the evening spent with Jace in puzzlement. They had gone to Oakland's waterfront area, the birthplace of the city, which centers around historic Jack London Square. Once there, she and Jace had wandered aimlessly through the ten blocks of landscaped malls and shops. Finally stopping to eat, they naturally chose a seafood restaurant, and enjoyed the sight of the lighted ships anchored in the Oakland Estuary while dining.

Laura made a determined effort to stay off controversial subjects, and although their conversation had remained almost totally impersonal, it hadn't hampered her enjoyment. After a while she even found herself relaxing in his presence, something she thought would be impossible under the circumstances.

Before leaving for home, Jace had insisted they stop and have a drink at the First and Last Chance Saloon. Built in 1880 from the remains of an old whaling ship, the building had been first a bunkhouse for oystermen, and later a saloon. Once inside, she was catapulted into the past. It was filled with photos and mementos of California author Jack London, for it was once one of his favorite haunts. As far as she had been concerned, she thought, a faint smile tugging at the corners of her mouth, they could have stayed all night, just soaking up the atmosphere.

She hadn't been surprised to find Jace extremely knowledgeable about Jack London. If there was one thing she was beginning to learn about him, it was that he was a voracious reader, his interests wide and varied.

Suddenly Laura glanced down at the clock beside the bed, remembering the suggestion Jace had made the night before. She just had time to shower and dress if she didn't want to waste the best part of the day. In her haste, she thumbed through the clothes closet, biting her lip in indecision. The spring sunlight pouring through the open draperies gave her a hint as to the day's warmth, so she settled for a spaghetti-strapped sundress in rusty brown, mainly for the convenience of the matching bodice-hugging jacket.

Placing an apron over her dress, she began fixing breakfast. She didn't see any dirty dishes in the sink, so she could safely assume Jace hadn't yet prepared his breakfast.

"I was going to take care of that!"

"Oh," she gasped, turning to face his imposing shape filling the doorway. "You startled me."

Jace chuckled, his eyes sparkling as he observed her indignant face. "I'd thought about taking you breakfast in bed. Wouldn't you have rather waited?"

A scathing retort was building, but she stopped herself from uttering it. Jace was in a good mood, and she didn't want to ruin the little accord existing between them over something so petty.

Smiling, she suggested he would be better off seating himself in the dining room and venting some of his frustrations on his breakfast. She heard his laughter as he departed, and a warmth spread throughout her body. Dishing up their plates, she found herself smiling nonsensically, but she couldn't care less. Today was a day for forgetting rancor and just enjoying herself, as she had last night.

It didn't take them long to eat and clear away the mess, and before she knew it, they were headed toward the wine country of Napa-Sonoma Valley. As they left the more familiar terrain behind, conversation lagged between them and they approached their destination, the Valley of the Moon, in silence. Low golden hills and higher mountains, scattered ranches, long lines of eucalyptus following the road, vineyards shimmering in the distant heat haze, and oak-studded meadows, kept Laura enthralled with the scenery.

The actual town of Glen Ellen came as a surprise to Laura. One moment they were surrounded by trees, and the next they had entered, quite literally, a glen, with creeks and homes tucked in mini-canyons.

Jace laughed at her surprise, turning toward her after stopping the car at the side of the road, to afford them a better view.

"It's hard to believe this place even exists," she breathed, her eyes roaming the terrain avidly.

"Yes, it was famous long before Jack London moved here."

"I didn't realize that."

"Not many people know that it was a popular vacation spot, served by two railroads. Glen Ellen was also a center for winemaking."

"Will we have time to visit some of the wineries?"

"We'll make time." He smiled, starting the car and heading toward the town. "Your wish is my command, my lady, and anyway, I need to restock the bar."

They enjoyed a scanty lunch in town before heading in the direction of the forty-eight-acre Jack London State Historic Park, which was located atop a rolling hill about a mile west of Glen Ellen. As they drove, they discussed the author, born in poverty in San Francisco, but raised in Oakland. He was possibly the best-known, best-read and best-loved American author of his time. Maybe, Jace remarked, this was because his books carried much of his own exuberance.

The author's enthusiasm for life was evident as they toured the House of Happy Walls, built by London's wife after his death, and the home she lived in until her own death nearly forty years later. Together they had traveled widely, by horseback to Oregon, to the South Seas and beyond, but the ranch Laura and Jace now visited had always been home to them.

One of their fondest dreams was a great twenty-six-room mansion they called Wolf House, built of native volcanic rock and redwood, with nine fireplaces, a court-yard, and room for the dozens of guests who came from all over the world to visit. Just weeks before they were to move in, the house burned in a mysterious fire, and they were never able to rebuild.

A marked trail led through woodlands of oak and madrona to ruins screened by redwoods. As she and Jace stood before the imposing shell, she couldn't help feeling a poignant sadness enveloping her. Her own shattered dreams were too new . . . too painful, and she turned away from the charred structure abruptly, not particularly caring if Jace followed or not.

As she trudged back up the path, she thought about the woman who had loved Jack London. The house she had spent thirty-nine years of her life in after her husband's death was a memorial to him . . . and she must have been desperately lonely. Cynically, Laura couldn't help speculating upon whether *he* would have given the rest of his life to fostering *her* memory.

Her earlier happy mood was completely overshadowed by depression, and Jace noticed the change as soon as he joined her. Without a word they began the drive back to the main highway, Laura's head averted from the sight of strong brown hands gripping the wheel. She wasn't in the right frame of mind to chatter unconcernedly as she had earlier, and she was thankful Jace respected her silence.

They drove for nearly an hour before Jace once more exited the highway. "We're going to stop at one of those wineries you wanted to visit," he explained before she had the chance to ask. "I thought maybe we'd have an early dinner before starting back for the wedding rehearsal," he continued, glancing at her inquiringly.

Laura agreed to his suggestion with a nod. To be fair, Jace was doing his best to entertain her, and she felt guilty for spoiling his enjoyment. It wasn't his fault that thoughts of their shaky marriage had filled her with such a tremendous sense of loss.

But she could never forgive Jace for covering up her father's affair—that was the root of the problem. As it was, she knew she could never trust his feelings for her, not if he could condone adultery. Her first husband had calmly left when he found someone willing to give him the material things in life he craved, but not before he had disgusted her by his affairs with other women. The possibility of Jace also discarding her eventually was, as far as she could see, only too real.

Although she couldn't honestly say she enjoyed her tour of the winery, it did prove to be the stimulus she needed to lift her emotions. She was fascinated by the winemaking process, especially the tasting that Jace had arranged beforehand. Obviously he had taken special trouble to bring her here, since dinner was served by prior reservation only.

The wedding rehearsal went smoothly, thanks to Cheryl's mother's efforts, and Laura threw herself into her role as matron of honor. She had been dreading the rehearsal, and the remarks people were bound to make about her own marriage, all week, but surprisingly she felt pleasantly relaxed during the drive home.

As they garaged the car, she felt a definite sense of homecoming. For the first time she felt as if she truly belonged as she entered the living room, but her satisfaction was short-lived when Jace turned to her.

"You're tired," he remarked quietly, studying her face in the dim light of the hall. "I'll lock up down here while you go on up to bed. You'll want to be rested for the wedding tomorrow."

Before she could protest his abruptness, he turned and entered the living room, leaving her standing at the foot of the stairs with a strong sensation of disappointment. She watched as he walked over to the bar, turning her head away from the sight of his disturbingly attractive body.

Feeling the way I do, how can I want him so badly? she

thought in bewilderment as she slowly climbed the stairs toward the lonely guest room. Instead of lessening, the attraction she felt toward him seemed to have increased. She had told herself over and over again how much she despised him for what he was doing. Why, then, were her heightened emotions still tearing her apart?

12

᠆᠆ᢁᢁᢁᢁᢁᢁᢁᢁᢁ᠆

Cheryl and Frank couldn't have had a more perfect day
for their wedding, Laura thought, throwing rice on the
fleeing couple. Cheryl looking heartbreakingly radiant,
Frank so very proud. . . . Laura felt tears forming behind
her lids as she watched them drive away.

As Jace's arm came around her, she turned to him with
a watery smile. "I'm so happy for them," she whispered.
"I hope with all my heart that they'll be happy together."

The muscles in his arm tensed just seconds before he
withdrew his arm from around her waist. As she saw the
brooding sadness in his eyes, she felt her heart drop.

"Yes," he muttered, beginning to walk with her to their
car. "Let's hope their love is strong enough to weather
the storms."

Without another word spoken between them, they
endured the happy celebration for their friends, while
inside Laura felt as if being at the festivities was almost a
sacrilege. Damn him! He makes me feel so guilty, and I
can't even understand why, she fumed. By the time they
reached home, she was in a turmoil. She avoided even

looking at Jace when she got out of the car, walking stiffly through the doorway and into the living room.

Laura stood nervously, watching as he removed his evening coat. The ringing of the phone caused her to jump. She went toward the telephone stand with jerky movements, but Jace was there before her.

"Hello!" A grayish pallor crept across the strong lines of his face, his next words shooting from his mouth with a staccato precision that caused a ball of fear to knot in Laura's stomach. "When?" he continued. "How bad? Yes, we'll be right there!"

She could feel her fingers trembling as she clutched at his sleeve. "What is it? What's wrong?"

Jace looked down at her, replacing the receiver and covering her hand with his own. "It's your father, Laura. He's had a heart attack. They've taken him to Kaiser. I told your mother we'd be there as soon as possible."

Jace led her into the bedroom, advising her to get undressed while he ran upstairs for a sweater and slacks for her to wear. She moved to obey him automatically, grateful that she wouldn't have to climb the stairs herself. The way her legs felt, she wouldn't make it!

He returned within moments, and she quickly slipped on the tan slacks and brown pullover sweater he had chosen. By the time she had changed into a comfortable pair of loafers, Jace was changed and waiting by the door.

The next hours were a nightmare she would never in her life care to repeat. When they arrived at Kaiser, it was to discover that her father was in the intensive-care unit, and upon entering the waiting area, they found her mother in a state of collapse.

While Laura held her, she sobbed out all her remorse

and guilt. Irene had just that day discovered the real reason for Darryl's frequent nights away from home. Far from having an affair, he had been coming to the hospital to have various tests completed, tests which proved him a likely candidate for open-heart surgery. The woman she had once spoken to had been a nurse from the hospital, calling to confirm his appointment.

"Oh, God, Laura!" Irene sobbed. "I was thinking such terrible things, when all along he was trying to protect me from the truth of his condition. He couldn't stand the thought of my having to endure months of fear and uncertainty. This morning he told me everything. . . ." she choked, taking a deep breath before trying to continue. "Th-then he went to lie down and . . . and . . ."

Laura's head lifted and her eyes locked with Jace's. The pity and concern she saw within their depths for both her and her mother unnerved her, and she felt her own eyes filling with tears. Oh, God, how she had misjudged the entire situation!

The doctor came and spoke to her mother, and when Irene hurriedly followed him into her father's room, Laura turned to Jace. "I . . . Is my father going to die?"

"Not if I can help it," he replied grimly. "Your parents have come to mean a lot to me, and I don't give up easily. Darryl's a tough old bird . . . he'll make it. The last few nights we've been going over the details of his business dealings so that I can take over the reins of the corporation while he takes a cruise and regains his strength. By the time he returns from a second honeymoon with your mother, he'll be rested, and I'm sure the surgery will turn out all right. The most important thing is for us to give them the support they'll need . . . together!"

When Irene returned, Laura could hardly believe the change that had taken place since she had entered her husband's room. She was standing proud and straight; her eyes, still glistening with tears, looked somehow radiant.

"He's going to be all right," she murmured, taking Jace and Laura by the hand. "The attack was a mild one and did very little damage, thank the good Lord. With a few weeks' rest and proper medication, the doctor assured us he would be strong enough for corrective surgery."

"Mother, c-can I see him?"

Irene nodded, her eyes softening when she looked at Laura. "He was asking for you, darling."

Swallowing the lump in her throat, she moved in the direction of her father's room. Quietly pushing the door open, she stepped forward until she stood looking down at the man who lay there with such uncharacteristic stillness. The shock of seeing him so still, so helpless, the closed lids with a faintly bluish cast, the gray pallor of skin usually vibrant with health—all contributed to the shaking sobs which wrenched her slender frame.

His hand moved across the pristine whiteness of the hospital sheets, and with a choked gasp Laura reached for its solid comfort.

"Daddy, I love you. I'm s-so sorry." It was the cry of the child she had been—the lonely, lost child who had longed, all those years ago, to be accepted and recognized by the only man in her life who had meant anything to her. She didn't really expect that recognition now, and

179

was startled when her fingers were gripped tightly. His eyes opened briefly, and a deep, lasting message passed between them, swelling Laura's heart with the love she had thought never to know.

"I . . . love you . . . Chicky!"

Jace was waiting for her when she stepped back into the corridor. His arms came around her in unspoken comfort, and Laura leaned her aching head on his chest.

"H-he said he . . . loves m-m . . ."

"It's all right, honey," Jace soothed. "This is a nightmare, but it'll soon be over."

Gentle hands on her hair were so comforting against her aching temples, she never wanted them to stop. Yet she couldn't accept this comfort from a man she had wronged so dreadfully. She had to ask for a forgiveness she didn't deserve, had to let him know that even while trying to convince herself she despised him, she had never, for one moment, stopped loving him.

The words were muffled against his chest, but she knew he heard by the tightening of his arms, which pulled her even closer to the warmth of his body.

"I . . . It was the same with my father," she whispered, her hands moving around his back and clenching against his shirt. "He called me Chicky. He hasn't called me that since I was little, and I'd forgotten that it was his special name for me. Oh, Jace! All these years I've blamed him for not caring enough, and yet even if he had tried, he wouldn't have been able to reach past the wall of resentment I placed around myself."

"Laura, don't torture yourself with useless regrets," he murmured, his lips warm against the dampness of her temple.

"But don't you see," she cried, leaning her head

backward until she could look into his eyes. "I almost did the same thing to you . . . to us. . . ."

"It wasn't your fault. I should have explained, but my damn pride reared its ugly head. I was just as much to blame for wanting you to love me enough to trust no matter what, and for that I need *your* forgiveness, Laura."

"You know something?" Laura asked the question almost absentmindedly, while a blessed sense of peace descended on her. "I'm not afraid, although I guess I should be. I know he's going to be all right . . . I know it!"

"That's right," he soothed. "You have nothing to fear from the future. When trouble comes, as it has now, we'll face it together. I'll be there to protect you when I can, and if I'm unable to prevent you from knowing pain, I'll share it with you."

Laura and Irene spent the next couple of weeks living out of the economy apartment Jace rented for them near the hospital. Every day saw her father stronger, and on the morning he received his release, Laura's hand was in his as he was wheeled out of the doors by an orderly, and deposited in Jace's car.

The next day her parents were leaving for the cruise Jace had insisted on, and her mother was as excited as a bride, her face flushed with happiness.

It was evening before they finally left her parents' house, and Laura felt, as she entered the living room of their own home, that she had lived through an eternity since she had been there last.

"I . . . I'm certainly glad to be home," she stammered, her eyes briefly meeting Jace's and sliding away from the demand she saw growing there. Suddenly she felt shy, unable to cope with the new tension which had been building between them over the past weeks. She had longed for the moment when they would be alone together, without the hampering presence of her mother, and yet, now that it was here, she found herself shying away from the vibrant gleam in his eyes.

"I . . . I think I'll take a shower."

A mocking smile creased his face, but he only nodded. "I've moved your things back into our room."

The warmth of the pounding water didn't do much to cool her heated flesh, but the sensuous feeling as it slid over her skin caused her to sigh with pleasure. Turning, she raised her arms over her head in a languid gesture, her eyes widening as the door opened and Jace stepped inside.

The needles of flowing hot water against her were like nothing compared to the flaming intensity of his gaze. For long moments he just watched her. With a muffled cry of embarrassment she started to lower her arms, catching her breath when her movement was prevented by his firm grip on her wrists.

Jace forced her arms upward, pressing her back against the coolness of the tile with the weight of his body. His mouth opened over hers, his tongue seeking and finding direction as it mingled with her own, and a swirling torrent of sensation rippled across her skin. The feeling of his damply matted hair against her breasts was driving her crazy as Jace moved against her, and she arched her back in an attempt to intensify the feeling, moaning low in her throat.

"Let's get out of here," he muttered. She noticed a

tremor in his hand as he reached to turn off the water, and a small laugh escaped her.

"I feel like a drowned rat."

"You look like one, too," he teased, ruffling her wet hair.

Wrapped in a daze of happiness, she watched while he began briskly rubbing the droplets of water from his body. He smoothed the thick luster of his silver-streaked hair with a comb, his eyes meeting hers in the mirror. She looked away in confusion.

"Here, let me do that!"

Jace's tone was husky as he reached over to remove the dryer from her hand. Her eyes closed blissfully as he gently drew a brush through the damp strands.

Before very long, cascading curls were fluffing around his hands. At his touch she felt a resurgence of trembling need, and she read a similar desire as their gazes locked together in the mirror. Shutting off the blow dryer and replacing it in the cabinet beneath the basin, he turned to her, his hand outstretched.

Without another word she allowed him to lead her into the shadowed bedroom. Her towel joined his on the carpet, and she was lifted into his arms, her head falling to his shoulder as if it were meant to be there.

They lay entwined on the bed, and Laura sighed with contentment, luxuriating in the silken feel of the sheets beneath her nakedness.

"Jace?"

"Mmmm," he answered, a contentment in his voice echoing her own.

"Nothing . . . just Jace," she replied, smiling at the inanity of the remark.

As he settled her more comfortably against him, she remembered all the misunderstandings, and shivered.

"Cold?"

Shaking her head negatively, she automatically reached upward to clutch at his shoulder. By using the past to hide behind, she had come so close to losing him . . . so close to never knowing this moment.

"Jace, I love you," she murmured against his skin, rubbing her cheek confidingly against the softly curling hairs of his chest. "I . . . I want you to know that I've never felt like this before. It isn't just the lovemaking . . ."

"I know, honey. Don't you think I feel the same?"

"I don't see how," she admitted. "You weren't the basket case I was."

His chest rose with his laughter, and she smiled quietly in the darkness. Snuggling even closer, she realized that deep inside herself she had always understood Jace's motives. She had suspected he would demand everything from her . . . and now that she was finally able to fill that demand, both physically and emotionally, she knew how right he had been. He didn't want lovemaking without love—it was only her own insecurities that had made her suspect that.

"I'll never deny you my trust again, Jace," she whispered against his neck. "I never want you to stop loving me."

"Fat chance," he muttered, turning and molding her body to his.

Suddenly she had had enough of the serious tone their conversation had taken. The touch of his skin against her had given her other ideas. Life could be so brief—as recent events had proved—and she had no intention of wasting another moment. She needed the hunger of his mouth, the blessed haven of his arms, to dispel forever the last lingering traces of the past.

"Jace?"

He groaned, his head falling backward against the pillow, trapping her hair underneath. "What now, woman?"

"Love me!"

He turned his head, his eyes filled with mock innocence. "I do love you!"

"I didn't mean that," she protested, her mouth an inviting pout as she moved sensuously against him.

Sighed words were lost in the possession of his seeking mouth as he obeyed her request eagerly. Spearing tongues added to her desire for closer contact, and she slid her hands upward over the hairy surface of his naked chest, hearing him groan low in his throat.

They were both having difficulty with their breathing before he finally lifted his lips from the parted softness of hers, and she smiled up at him, her own face gentle with love. He drew in his breath sharply, shaking his head as if to clear it.

"Honey, there's so much I want to say . . . but I can't find the words." He sighed, his hand caressing her cheek wonderingly.

"Not now . . . just love me . . . love me," she moaned, circling his neck with trembling hands.

"Not now," he promised, his mouth smoothing a delicious trail across her throat. "Now I have to love you."

Her spirit rose joyously to meet his. His hands played with her body as if every curve and angle were an intricate melody which delighted his fingers. Her own hands took infinite pleasure in the feel of his flesh, until his eyes met the shimmering promise of hers.

As their glances locked together, she shivered at the sudden wildness in his face. Again his mouth coaxed her lips to part for his entry, and she responded wildly, her whole body coming alive in his arms.

"Yes," he moaned, as her hands began taking the initiative, wandering intently over him. "Oh, God! Touch me . . . move with me!"

She obeyed his commands eagerly. She shivered anew when her palms slid against the bareness of his smooth skin, his mouth muffling her delighted moan when he began duplicating the caresses on her own heated flesh.

Together they moved higher and higher, each straining to reach the shelter of their haven together. Bodies and minds fused, making them forever inseparable, and as Laura's floating spirit touched the shores of their secret place, she knew that only together would they ever be truly free.

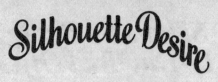

Coming Next Month

Not Even For Love by Erin St. Claire

When a misunderstanding threatened to drive
them apart, the memory of their passion drove
Jordan to convince Reeves of the truth. His misty
green eyes and sensual mouth had lifted her to
peaks of ecstasy she could never forget.

Make No Promises by Sherry Dee

Even though Cassie was engaged to another
man, she was instantly attracted to Steele
Malone. He waged a passionate war on her
senses, defying her emotions and lulling her
body with primitive pleasures.

Moment In Time by Suzanne Simms

She knew Tyler expected a man to build his
treasured dam, but Carly was a fully qualified
civil engineer. What began as a battle of wills
blazed anew in the Santa Fe sunset, a flashfire
passion which consumed them both.

Whenever I Love You by Alana Smith

Diana Nolan was Treneau Cosmetics' new
goddess of beauty. Paul Treneau was the boss
who whisked her away to his Hawaiian paradise
for "business." But she had ignited in him a
spark of desire fated to burn out of control.

YOU'LL BE SWEPT AWAY
WITH SILHOUETTE DESIRE

$1.75 each

1 ☐ CORPORATE AFFAIR
Stephanie James

2 ☐ LOVE'S SILVER WEB
Nicole Monet

3 ☐ WISE FOLLY
Rita Clay

4 ☐ KISS AND TELL
Suzanne Carey

5 ☐ WHEN LAST WE LOVED
Judith Baker

6 ☐ A FRENCHMAN'S KISS
Kathryn Mallroy

Silhouette Desire

Now Available

Corporate Affair by Stephanie James

Kalinda had come to Colorado determined to avenge a lost love. But she was shaken by Rand Alastair who conquered and claimed her wounded heart.

Love's Silver Web by Nicole Monet

When Jace's lips, hot and passionate, came down on hers, Laura was overwhelmed with desire. It was just a matter of time before he possessed her, body and soul.

Wise Folly by Rita Clay

Seven years had not dimmed Diana's desire for Noah. How could she deny him now, when he gave her everything she ever longed for and more?

Kiss And Tell by Suzanne Carey

Jenna tried to free her mind of Duke Tyrell. But one moonlit night haunted her, when Duke had captured her heart and mesmerized her senses with love.

When Last We Loved by Judith Baker

Even the glitter and flash of Nashville's country music world couldn't compete with the dizzying rapture Cassie felt in Hoyt Temple's arms.

A Frenchman's Kiss by Kathryn Mallory

In the dark, ripe fields of grapes that stretched out around them, Jean Paxton abandoned herself to the searing kisses of a Frenchman who made her forget . . .

Dear Reader:
Please take a few moments to fill out this questionnaire. It will help us give you more of the Desires you'd like best.

Mail to: **Karen Solem**
Silhouette Books
1230 Ave. of the Americas, New York, N.Y. 10020

1. How did you obtain **LOVE'S SILVER WEB?**
10-1 ☐ **Bookstore**   -6 ☐ **Newsstand**
  -2 ☐ **Supermarket**   -7 ☐ **Airport**
  -3 ☐ **Variety/discount store** -8 ☐ **Book Club**
  -4 ☐ **Department store**   -9 ☐ **From a friend**
  -5 ☐ **Drug store**   -0 ☐ **Other:** _____
                                        (write in)

2. How many Silhouette Desires have you read including this one?
   (circle one number) 11- **1 2 3 4 5 6**

3. Overall how would you rate this book?
12-1 ☐ **Excellent** -2 ☐ **Very good**
  -3 ☐ **Good**   -4 ☐ **Fair** -5 ☐ **Poor**

4. Which elements did you like best about this book?
13-1 ☐ **Heroine** -2 ☐ **Hero** -3 ☐ **Setting** -4 ☐ **Story line**
  -5 ☐ **Love scenes** -6 ☐ **Ending** -7 ☐ **Other Characters**

5. Do you prefer love scenes that are
14-1 ☐ **Less explicit than**   -2 ☐ **More explicit than**
     in this book   **in this book**
            -3 ☐ **About as explicit as in this book**

6. What influenced you most in deciding to buy this book?
15-1 ☐ **Cover** -2 ☐ **Title** -3 ☐ **Back cover copy**
  -4 ☐ **Recommendations** -5 ☐ **You buy all Silhouette Books**

7. How likely would you be to purchase other Silhouette Desires in the future?
16-1 ☐ **Extremely likely**   -3 ☐ **Not very likely**
  -2 ☐ **Somewhat likely**   -4 ☐ **Not at all likely**

8. Have you been reading...
17-1 ☐ **Only Silhouette Romances**
  -2 ☐ **Mostly Silhouette Romances**
  -3 ☐ **Mostly one other romance** _____
                                    (write one in)
  -4 ☐ **No one series of romance in particular**

9. Please check the box next to your age group.
18-1 ☐ **Under 18**   -3 ☐ **25-34**   -5 ☐ **50-54**
  -2 ☐ **18-24**   -4 ☐ **35-49**   -6 ☐ **55 +**

10. Would you be interested in receiving a romance newsletter? If so please fill in your name and address.

Name _____

Address _____

City _____ State _____ Zip _____

        19 ___ 20 ___ 21 ___ 22 ___ 23 ___